# "I'd never let anything happen to you."

Kate believed him absolutely. She lifted a hand to his face. At the same time, a dark cloud drifted across the night sky, revealing a crescent of moon. The silvery stream of light illuminated his face, allowing her to see the way his eyes had darkened again to that thrilling, terrifying, stormy-sea hue.

Alec let out a breath, then, in one violent motion, yanked her against him. Feeling his rock-hard arousal, knowing that she'd caused his dramatic response, fanned the flames of her own desire even higher, and this time her soft cry was one of wonder. Of need.

As his mouth closed over hers, not gently, Alec was consumed with urgency. He forgot gentleness, surrendered control to the wild warrior within as he plundered, taking what he wanted and demanding more.

He'd gone from merely tasting to devouring in a single rapid-fire heartbeat. His hands were everywhere, cruising over her face, tangling in her hair, diving below the thigh-length cotton nightshirt to race over her body with an incendiary touch.

For a man who'd always prided himself on his control, Alec was discovering that restraint was absolutely impossible whenever he was with this woman....

Dear Reader,

In 1999 Harlequin will celebrate its 50th anniversary in North America. Canadian publishing executive Richard Bonnycastle founded the company in 1949. Back then they published a wide variety of American and British paperbacks—from mysteries and Westerns to classics and cookbooks. In later years the company focused on romance exclusively, and today Harlequin is the world's leading publisher of series romance fiction. Our books are sold in over 100 countries and published in more than twenty-three languages. Love stories are a universal experience!

Harlequin Temptation is delighted to help celebrate this very special anniversary. We're throwing a bachelor auction...and you're invited! Join five of our leading authors as they each put a sexy hero on the auction block. Sparks fly when the heroines get a chance to bid on their fantasy men.

Longtime favorite Temptation author JoAnn Ross sets the stage for the bachelor auction in the romantic, sexy *Mackenzie's Woman*. JoAnn has written over fifty novels and has an incredible 8 million copies of her books in print. Truly she is one of Harlequin's shining stars.

Each month we strive to bring you the very best stories and writers. And we plan to keep doing that for the next fifty years!

Happy anniversary,

Birgit Davis-Todd
Senior Editor
Harlequin Temptation

# JoAnn Ross
# MACKENZIE'S WOMAN

TORONTO • NEW YORK • LONDON
AMSTERDAM • PARIS • SYDNEY • HAMBURG
STOCKHOLM • ATHENS • TOKYO • MILAN • MADRID
PRAGUE • WARSAW • BUDAPEST • AUCKLAND

ISBN 0-373-25817-8

MACKENZIE'S WOMAN

Copyright © 1999 by JoAnn Ross.

This edition published by arrangement with Harlequin Books S.A.

® and TM are trademarks of the publisher. Trademarks indicated with ® are registered in the United States Patent and Trademark Office, the Canadian Trade Marks Office and in other countries.

Printed in U.S.A.

# Prologue

DURING HIS ADVENTUROUS thirty-five years, Alec Mackenzie had talked his way out of a potentially deadly encounter with a tribe of headhunters in New Guinea, wrestled a crocodile in the Australian outback and survived a Sahara sirocco for five days with only a package of beef jerky and a canteen of water for sustenance and a nasty-tempered camel named Clyde to block the blowing sand. But of all the perils he'd managed to survive, none had possessed such potential for danger as this one.

Oh, the Grand Ballroom of the world renowned Waldorf-Astoria admittedly might seem, at first glance, far more hospitable than the no-man's lands he usually hung out in. The round tables were draped in snowy damask and adorned with elaborate, sweet-smelling floral centerpieces. Dark green bottles of champagne were nestled in ice, glasses continually filled by formally dressed waiters. The gilt chandeliers glowed overhead like a thousand suns and the expensive perfumes worn by women clad in sparkly gowns made the lushly appointed ballroom smell like the gardens at Versailles.

Diamonds glittered like the ice surrounding the champagne bottles, emeralds and rubies sparkled, gold gleamed.

But Alec knew, better than most, that appearances could be deceiving. The truth was that he'd rather be thrown stark naked into a school of archaeologist-eating piranhas than to be standing here on this stage, dressed in black tie, allowing more than a thousand pairs of avid female eyes to ogle him.

The bright lights at his feet and the flashing of light from all those crystal beads and sequins blinded Alec. But he didn't need the sense of sight to know exactly where the woman who'd gotten him into this mess was sitting. He'd always had internal radar where Katherine Jeanne Campbell was concerned. Just as he'd always had a soft spot in his heart for the head-strong, frustrating, but oh, so luscious female.

Which was, of course, partly why he'd allowed her to rope him into this charity gig in the first place. But it was only one of the reasons, Alec reminded himself with a hot surge of masculine resolve.

The charity auction being held in the Big Apple to celebrate Heart Books's fiftieth anniversary was admittedly for a good cause. As a bestselling adventure novelist, Alec certainly had a vested interest in building his audience, and no one could fault the romance publisher's goal of raising funds to assist various literacy agencies. However, since he was, thanks to both the treasures he'd uncovered and his books, a wealthy man, it would have been a lot easier just to have his accountant write out a hefty donation check.

But oh, no, that would have been too damn easy, Alec thought darkly. He tried to remind himself that he'd spent his entire life not trusting things that came too easily. Still, the idea of being auctioned off to the highest female bidder—like some bedouin's rangy goat!—rankled.

It didn't help that he had only himself to blame, since in the end, it had been his choice to put himself on the literacy auction block. But only because he was a man with a plan.

The first time he'd seen his Kate, across the proverbial crowded room, Alec had felt exactly the same way he'd felt when he'd caught his first glimpse of the *Maria Isabella*. After years of searching, he'd found the galleon lying silent at the bottom of the Caribbean, her treasure trove of Spanish gold his for the taking. When he'd first seen Kate she'd been wearing a prim little dress-for-success, pinstriped gray suit that, while not the least bit sexy in cut or color, had set off her red hair and revealed smooth, slender legs.

*Mine,* he'd thought instantly. He'd wanted her with a passion that Alec might have found unnerving if he'd taken time to think about it. Which he hadn't. The only thing that had been in his fevered mind that night was that he intended to have the flame-haired female. Which he had. Again and again. But when morning had dawned, he'd made the biggest mistake of his life: after a blistering argument, he'd let her get away.

But not tonight, he vowed with grim determination.

As the emcee introduced him with embarrassing hyperbole, relating his expeditions in a breathless way that had him sounding like an exaggerated version of Indiana Jones, Alec ran his finger around the inside of the overly starched collar and tried to remember the last time he'd worn a tie, let alone a tux. Ah, his cousin John's wedding, which had been what, seven, eight years ago? Just one more thing Kate was going to have to pay for, he vowed.

At least he'd cut down the bidding pool. Suspecting that most females were suckers for grand romantic gestures, he'd purposely chosen a date he figured the majority of attendees would willingly pass on. After all, how many women would be all that eager to go on an archaeological dig in icy Lapland? There wasn't a lot of demand for designer dresses and expensive scents north of the arctic circle.

Surely prospective bidders would prefer a romantic candlelight dinner at some trendy city restaurant to caribou stew, canned beans and a dessert of freeze-dried peaches from his store of military surplus meals served up in a tent staked out on some far distant iceberg.

The emcee extolled his so-called attributes—his fame, his fortune.... His body, which he'd always considered adequate for what he needed it to do, but she insisted on calling cover-model hunky. In the mean time, Alec indulged in a fantasy of all the ways he planned to collect on the long overdue debt.

Oh yes, he thought with grim satisfaction, Kate had enjoyed her little dance. But as soon as this damn charity bachelor auction was over, they both knew that it would be time—way past time—for her to pay the piper. And Alec was more than ready to collect.

An archaeologist who delved into ancient civilizations while searching the world for hidden treasures, Alec had always believed important lessons could be learned from the past. And in Kate's case, if past experience was anything to go by, the woman he'd come to think of as his Achilles' heel would relish every hot sexy moment. As would he.

He may have begun this adventure seeking revenge, but during the past few days, his goal had changed. Oh, he still intended to have her. But not for any brief hot affair.

He'd come here to New York tonight and was putting himself through this embarrassing dog-and-pony show for one reason and one reason only—to get his woman back. In his bed, and in his life, where she damn well belonged. Forever.

# 1

*Heart Books New York Offices*
*One month earlier*

"WHAT WE NEED is a hero."

The statement, tossed out in the middle of the meeting, caused every head in the conference room to turn toward K. J. Campbell.

"Excuse me?" A vice president of public relations arched a blond brow.

"For the auction," K.J. qualified. "We need a hero."

"We have a plethora of bachelors signed up for the literacy auction. In fact," the vice president said with obvious pride, "we've just managed to sign up Jeffrey Winston III."

"Terrific," K.J. muttered. "That's all we need, another banker."

"A millionaire banker," Molly Stewart, who was sitting beside K.J. at the long, hand-carved mahogany conference table, murmured. Although the editor's tone was mild, everyone in the room knew it was a warning to her best friend. Ticking off vice presidents was not exactly conducive to career advancement.

But it was K.J.'s nature to speak her mind, and although she honestly tried not to rock boats, the buttoned-up corporate world could never change nature. "Winston's got bucks," she agreed. "And I'll admit he's kind of cute, in an uptight, wing-tipped, Harvard Business School way."

"And don't forget the fabulous date he's offering." A representative from the art department entered the conversation. "A champagne dinner for two and a moonlit cruise aboard his yacht is a wonderfully romantic evening." The twenty-something woman sighed, just thinking about it.

"It's ordinary," K.J. complained. "It's been done a million times in a million romances. And when you get right down to it, if you take away his bucks, Winston's just an ordinary, run-of-the-mill guy with a great wardrobe. Let's not forget, people, who we are. And what we do."

On a roll now, K.J. stood up and began to pace, her forest green silk skirt twirling around her knees when she reached the window and spun around to face them all again.

"We're Heart Books. Our name is synonymous with romance all over the world. And while I agree that the bachelor auction is a great way to raise money for charity—"

"I'm so delighted you approve," the editorial director murmured dryly.

"Oh, I do." Intent on making her point, K.J. decided to overlook the tinge of sarcasm in the cultured voice. "Absolutely. But I woke up in the middle of the night and realized we've overlooked what we're really about."

"I have no doubt you're about to tell us what, precisely, that is," the vice president said coolly.

"You're right. I am." She stopped in front of a table-top-size bronze reproduction of *The Kiss* and paused for dramatic effect. "We may be in the romance business. But we don't really sell romance." Her gaze swept the room. "What we're actually selling is hunks."

"Which we have in abundance for the auction," Lisa Harding, senior editor, noted.

"True. Granted, a lot of the men signed up so far fit the category of hunks. But too many of them are still the kind of regular, everyday guys you can meet at the office."

"Not this office," Molly murmured.

K.J. huffed a frustrated breath. "Not everyone works in a building overrun with females. My point is that you can throw a wine cork in any upscale bar in the city after work and hit a dozen guys just like the bachelors we lined up so far.

"What we're missing, ladies and gentleman," she added, smiling at the outnumbered, lone male in the room as if hoping to win over his vote, "is a true-to-life hero. A man who's larger than life, someone women all over the world would fantasize about—"

"Someone like this?" a woman from marketing asked, holding up the hardcover novel she'd been reading earlier while waiting for everyone to show up in the conference room.

As she took in Alec Mackenzie's author photo on the back of the dustcover, K.J.'s breath clogged in her lungs. Instead of a studio shot, the casual photograph had been taken outdoors with the author wearing a rumpled khaki shirt that looked as if it had been washed on rocks in some far distant stream. Pyramids loomed in the background.

The subject was squinting because of the bright sun overhead, the lines fanning out from his gunmetal gray eyes adding character, not age, and his jet-black hair—the color of a moonless night over the Scottish moors—was ruffled, not by the electric fans used for similar effect during romance cover shoots, but by an actual desert wind.

*Now you've done it*, the puritanical censor that lived in the back of her mind and spoke with her grandmother's voice piped up. Proving that some things—and some people—were impossible to escape, the voice had popped into her head shortly after her grandmother's funeral.

"This guy has hero written all over him," the marketing woman pointed out unnecessarily.

"Surely you're not actually suggesting getting Alec Mackenzie for our auction?" The publicity vice president's astonished tone echoed the expressions on nearly all the faces in the room—a combination of impatience and disbelief.

"Why not?" Molly asked, obviously getting in the spirit of things. "K.J. has a point. We do need a guy who's a hero. And Mackenzie's a real-life Indiana Jones. I read in *Publishers Weekly* that he's one adventure writer whose female readership equals his male audience. And I can't believe anyone thinks that's because millions of women are all that interested in buried artifacts."

"Actually, his stories are quite gripping," the marketing woman argued, reaching out to reclaim her book from K.J. "And he doesn't exactly look for artifacts. He's more of a treasure hunter."

"That may be," Molly agreed as K.J. handed the thick novel over. "But are you reading that novel because you've always had a burning desire to learn about sunken Spanish galleons, or because you're lusting over the hero of the adventure, world-renowned archaeologist Jake Germaine?"

The woman flushed, just a little, but enough to make Molly's point. "Jake's a complex character," she insisted. "Mackenzie has done an admirable job of fleshing him out, revealing more of his personality with each book."

"He damn well should know the guy pretty well," Molly said. "Since it's common knowledge that the adventures of the intrepid, drop-dead-sexy, fictional treasure hunter, Jake Germaine, are more autobiography than fiction. We'd have women standing in line to buy tickets."

"I'll admit that Mackenzie would be not only the icing, but the candles on our fiftieth-anniversary cake," the editorial director agreed cautiously. A reluctant, but speculative gleam lit up her eyes. "But how do you suggest getting him to agree to such a thing?"

"It wouldn't hurt to just ask him right out. The worst he could do would be to say no."

"It might be worth a try, if we could find him. Even when he's not in some far-off corner of the world, the man's ridiculously reclusive," the publicity vice president said. "I had lunch with his publisher's PR guy a couple weeks ago and he was drinking doubles because Mackenzie had just turned down an offer to appear on *Oprah.*"

That remarkable news earned a chorus of surprised murmurs from all of the assembled staff but K.J.

"We still shouldn't give up," Molly insisted. "Maybe he'll fall for the literacy charity angle. After all, the more people who can read, the more people there are who'll buy his books."

"He'll never go for it," the publicity person warned. "I tell you, for a man who could probably sell another hundred thousand copies on a book tour on sex appeal alone, Mackenzie's reported to be dead set against public appearances. Besides, the guy's a poster boy for wanderlust. How do you suggest finding him?"

"Good question." Molly turned toward K.J. "Maybe you can give it a try. Didn't you get to know him at a conference last year?"

"Well, yes," K.J. admitted.

*Don't admit to a thing*, her inner scold advised sternly.

Realizing that she'd made a major mistake by speaking up in the first place, K.J. tried to follow that admonition. "But it's not as if—"

"You actually know Alec Mackenzie?" The editorial director cut off K.J.'s planned demurral.

"We've met," she admitted reluctantly. Nervous at even the most remote prospect of seeing Alec again, K.J. began toying with the monogrammed sterling silver Mont Blanc pen she'd received from her grandmother when she'd graduated from Sarah Lawrence eight years earlier.

"I thought you said you two had become friends," Molly said.

"That's not exactly right," K.J. hedged.

"Friendly enough that he might agree to a request from you?" the editorial director asked.

"I don't know." K.J. drew in a halting breath as her mind whirled frantically, trying to decide exactly how much she'd have to admit to. "I suppose I could try," she said without enthusiasm.

*I can't believe you said that!*

The alarmed voice reverberated around inside K.J.'s head like ricocheting bullets. The top came off her pen, allowing the spring to fly across the room. With all eyes on her flushed face, no one seemed to notice. Indeed, it would have been possible to hear a paper clip drop in the hush that had come over the conference room at that declaration.

"So you really are friends?" the marketing woman asked incredulously.

"Of sorts." That was such an out-and-out lie. K.J. could almost envision her Scots Calvinist ancestors spinning in their graves. "Friends" was definitely not the way to describe her relationship with Alec Mackenzie. Not in the beginning and definitely not now.

"Good enough friends that you can track him down?" the editorial director asked, not bothering to hide her skepticism.

K.J. was wishing the man's name hadn't come up in the first place. But she could have just denied having ever met Alec. And there was no reason why she'd needed to imply they had any type of relationship.

*Well, this certainly isn't the first time you've behaved impulsively where that man is concerned.*

Unfortunately, she thought with an inner groan, that was too true. Now the only thing left to do was to brazen it out.

Besides, she thought with a sudden burst of pent-up temper, Alec owed her. And if she could get him to agree to take part in the charity event, she might even be promoted to a senior slot. Which would, in turn, make her less likely to spend every weekend reading through the slush pile.

Not that she really minded reading all those unsolicited manuscripts that flooded into the offices every day; after all, it was thrilling when you stumbled across a sparkling diamond among all those lumps of coal. But it would be nice to have a little free time to work in her darkroom for a change.

Although photography had always been her first love, her paternal grandmother, with whom she'd gone to live after her parents' death when she was nine, had not been at all encouraging about K.J. following in her father's career footsteps. Helen Campbell, whose husband's family had made a fortune on Wall Street buying up stock for pennies on the dollar after the crash of 1929, had died last year in her sleep at the ripe old age of ninety-nine.

Before her death, she'd never missed an opportunity to remind K.J. that her father's inappropriate passion for photography had gotten not only himself killed on Mount Everest, but his wife, as well. That tragic avalanche was how the orphaned K.J. had ended up living with the woman George Campbell had been estranged from for nearly two decades before his untimely death.

From the first day she'd arrived at the Campbell Long Island estate, K.J. had done her best to please her rigid grandmother. She'd traded in her ragged, comfortable sneakers for black patent-leather Mary Janes, watched her beloved T-shirts and blue jeans being boxed away for Goodwill, and even silently submitted to having what her grandmother referred to as her "wild hooligan" hair coated with rotten-egg-smelling junk that turned it as straight as rainwater every six months. Only when she'd escaped to college had it been allowed to grow back into its riotous mass of light auburn curls.

She'd majored in English on a whim, since her grandmother refused to pay for photography classes and K.J. had always enjoyed reading. The fact that her mother had been an editor—indeed, the editor who had first discovered, then married, photographer George Campbell—made her feel closer to the parent she'd never stopped loving.

After graduation, K.J. had taken the job at the romance publisher, planning to stay only a few months, until she could support herself with the photographs she'd actually begun to sell.

A self-taught photographer who'd inherited her father's talented eye, she lacked the connections to the top galleries. Which was why, since she had an unfortunate addiction to eating at least one meal a day, she'd moved onto the editorial track.

Which wasn't all that much of a sacrifice, she reminded herself now. After all, most days she enjoyed her work. And after the art director had introduced her to a few of the photographers who shot the romance novel covers, some of them had invited her to Saturday morning shoots. K.J. willingly volunteered to change film, move light screens, anything to gain the technical skills she lacked. Recently, she'd even had a couple of minor showings, where colorful photographs of city street scenes had sold out.

"I suppose I could try to track Alec down," she agreed now with more enthusiasm than she was feeling.

That was all it took. The decision to have K.J. Campbell track down Alec Mackenzie and request that he take part in their anniversary bachelor auction was unanimous.

*You'll be sorry, girl.*

As they moved on to other new business, K.J. didn't hear another word of the meeting. Her internal scold's warning had her wondering what on earth she'd gotten herself into. She also had the strangest feeling she could hear her boisterous father laughing at her predicament.

"Okay, shoot," Molly demanded. It was after work and the two friends were having an early dinner in a

Chinatown restaurant. "Why did you get so upset when I brought up you having met Alec Mackenzie?"

"I don't know what you're talking about." K.J. slid her chopsticks out of their paper wrapper.

"You went so pale your freckles showed. We've been best friends for six years," Molly reminded her. She began spreading hot mustard on an egg roll. "There's something you haven't told me about the guy, isn't there?"

Stalling for time, K.J. picked up a piece of sesame chicken and popped it into her mouth. It was her favorite item on the menu. Tonight it tasted like dust. What in the world had she gotten herself into?

"You're right," she said with a sigh when she'd finished chewing.

She put her chopsticks down and rubbed her temples, where a headache that began as a twinge during the fateful meeting was now reaching blinding proportions. She could almost imagine some maniacal midget inside her head, pounding a huge brass gong like the one that took up most of the small entry at the front of the restaurant.

"I should have told you. It's just that it's a bit complicated."

"The best things in life often are."

The topic, along with her friend's probing look, had made her mouth go dry. K.J. took a long drink of wine, hoping it would help. It didn't.

"Okay, you're right. I did meet him last year. At that writers' conference in Las Vegas. The one you were scheduled to attend before you came down with that horrible cold."

"My ears were so stuffed up I was afraid they'd explode before the plane hit cruising altitude."

"Well, if you'll recall, I spoke on the larger-than-life

attributes of a romance hero. Alec was scheduled to give a workshop on research methods, but it was a huge conference, and since he arrived too late to make the welcoming cocktail party, we didn't actually run into each other until the closing banquet."

Molly was looking at K.J. over the rim of her wineglass, openly transfixed. "If this were published by our romance company, sparks would have started flying the minute you met."

"It was more than sparks." K.J. sighed again and shook her head, which only made it ache more. "Actually, it was more of a nuclear explosion. I have no memory of leaving the banquet. All I remember was being excruciatingly bored while politely listening to a play-by-play account of an autobiographical romance between a butcher and the ghost of a supermarket-produce-department manager who'd tragically died in the store's juicing machine—which, of course, the would-be author assured me would be a bestseller. I happened to glance across the room and find the most intensely passionate man I'd ever seen standing in the doorway of the banquet room."

"You could tell he was passionate from all the way across the room?" Molly asked disbelievingly.

"Absolutely." Even after all these months, K.J. felt the fire flare in her blood at the memory of that riveting moment when her entire world had tilted so dangerously on its axis. "And I realize it sounds like some fictional reaction from one of our books, but I swear, when his eyes met mine, I felt shivers all through my body."

"They always turn the air-conditioning down too low in hotels."

"But I wasn't cold. In fact, as I stared at the fire in his gray eyes as he walked toward me, I felt as if I were about to burst into flames. I couldn't speak. I couldn't even think. Which I suppose helps explain why, when he took hold of my hand as if he had every right to, I walked out of that ballroom with him."

*That was your second mistake. Your first was not running the first time you saw that treasure-hunting rogue.*

Molly refilled both their glasses. Her intelligent eyes widened as comprehension dawned. "Are you telling me that you—a woman who could easily be the poster girl for safe sex—actually slept with Alec Mackenzie?"

K.J. closed her blue eyes and held the glass against her throbbing temple. "That's precisely what I'm telling you," she murmured reluctantly. "I did sleep with Alec. But only after I married him."

# 2

*Somewhere in the jungles of South America*

"YOU KNOW WHAT YOU NEED?" the deep male voice inquired out of the blue.

"No. But I expect you're going to tell me," Alec muttered as he studied the ancient piece of parchment.

"You need to get laid."

That claim garnered his reluctant attention. Alec lifted his eyes to his best, and, when you came right down to it, his only friend, who was seated across the rickety wooden table from him. "That's your opinion. Actually, what I need is a dowser."

"And what is that?"

"A guy with a pointed stick who finds water."

"This adventure has already extended into the monsoon season," Rafael Santos noted. "I would think you already have more water than you know what to do with."

Alec scowled at that idea as the ancient generator-run paddle fan over his head, which was actually working today, turned lazily, doing little to cool the moisture-laden air. The plan had been to find the barge before the rainy season turned the entire jungle to mud. Unfortunately, he'd learned the hard way that expeditions didn't always work out as planned.

"It's not water I'd want him to find."

"Ah." Rafael nodded. "These dowsers can also find gold?"

"Not that I know of. But there's damn well gotta be a first time."

Alec glared back down at the ancient map he'd run across in a little shop in Barcelona specializing in old books. It had been in a leather-bound log allegedly belonging to a Spanish ship captain who'd returned from the New World with a fantastic tale of a barge loaded with Inca gold lost in the Andes.

According to the log, a landslide caused by the drenching rains had killed most of the conquistadors on the expedition. And buried a king's ransom in stolen booty.

If the log entry was to be believed, and instinct, along with a lot of follow-up research, had assured Alec it could be, the landslide had also closed off the Amazonian tributary and covered the barge and its precious cargo with tons of mud and silt. Inevitably, the jungle had reclaimed the land and the gold. For now.

"Why don't you give it a break?" Rafael asked, casting a glance across the cantina, which was little more than a lean-to surrounded by lush green plants and every species of tree known to man. "Sonia has been eyeing you all evening, and if she pulls that blouse down any lower, every man in the place is going to owe you a huge debt of gratitude." He grinned. "Take the willing wench to bed, Alec. Work off your sexual frustrations. And perhaps, with your body satisfied and your head cleared, the answer to your puzzle will appear tomorrow."

Alec looked at the voluptuous barmaid currently bent over a table, wiping away spilled beer. Her breasts were lush, golden and threatening to pop out

of the top of her low-necked cotton blouse at any moment. "The idea's admittedly tempting."

Especially since Sonia had made it clear, from the
first day he'd arrived in Santa Clara, that he would be
more than welcome in her bed. Alec sighed and took a
long pull on the brown beer bottle. "But in case you've
forgotten, I'm a married man."

"By law," his friend conceded. "But as I've been
telling you, it would be an easy enough matter to get
an annulment."

"And I keep telling you that an annulment isn't an
option."

"One night of passion does not make a marriage,"
Rafael argued, not for the first time. As an attorney, he
knew his case law. "Besides, there are other grounds
you could use besides nonconsummation. In case
you've forgotten, your blushing bride lied through her
pretty white teeth to you, then ran off."

"I haven't forgotten anything about that misadven-
ture," Alec grumbled.

Not that amazing, hit-by-lightning feeling he'd
never believed in until he'd first seen Katherine Jeanne
Campbell. Nor the hours they'd spent in the hotel bar,
her seeming to hang on his every word as he'd gone
on and on about this missing Inca gold he was determined to recover.

He certainly hadn't forgotten their marriage, which
may have taken less than ten minutes for the minister
to perform, but had damn well been legal by all the
laws of Nevada. He remembered in vivid detail every
sensual moment of that long, love-filled night when
he'd discovered, for the first time in his thirty-four
years, the true meaning of passion.

Nor had he forgotten the furious argument the following morning. Or the words of goodbye his bride

had written on hotel stationery and left on his pillow. Okay, admittedly he'd stormed out of the hotel room first. But she should have known that he had every intention of coming back once he'd cooled off. And given her time to see the light.

"What the woman did is, legally, abandonment, which is all you need to be a free man." Rafael was still arguing his case when Alec dragged his mind back to the present.

"I'm not getting an annulment."

Although he knew that Rafael—and anyone else who might hear the story of his ill-fated, too-brief marriage—would think him crazy, Alec remained convinced that one of these days Kate would come to her senses, realize her mistake, return to him, apologize for her hasty behavior and beg his forgiveness.

Oh yes, he thought as he took another, longer pull on the bottle, the idea of his red-haired bride on her knees was definitely an appealing fantasy.

When he realized that Sonia was smiling across the tavern at him, her lush ripe mouth sending a gilt-edged invitation, Alec tugged his rebellious lips from their unconscious grin back into his earlier scowl.

Sonia shook her dark head with obvious feminine pique and returned to scrubbing the table with more force than necessary, the action starting those magnificent breasts to swaying again in a way that had nearly every male in the cantina holding his breath. Every male but Alec.

Unfortunately, he thought with not a little regret, the provocative sight didn't arouse him in the least. Because his body—like his mind—had stayed focused on one woman all these months.

Oh yes, when their paths did finally cross again, he would benevolently forgive his wife. Then he had

every intention of catching up for lost time by making
mad passionate love to her until she was hoarse from
screaming his name and limp and drained from
countless orgasms.

And then, after he'd finally satiated his own gut-
grinding need, he was going to let her experience exactly how it felt to be the one who was walked out on.

*New York City*
"MARRIED?" Molly stared at K.J. in disbelief. "You've
got to be kidding."

"Believe me, there's nothing funny about it." Not
now, and especially not then, K.J. thought glumly.
"Well, there was one thing."

"What?"

"We were married by Merlin."

"Merlin?"

"You know, King Arthur's magician."

"Now I know you're lying."

"It's true. The hotel was one of those theme things—
a castle with moats and jesters and jousting knights.
Apparently a lot of people find it romantic to
exchange vows in the Camelot Cathedral dressed in
medieval costumes."

"The idea of Alec Mackenzie in a velvet doublet and
tights is just too depressing to contemplate."

"Oh, we didn't wear costumes. But we showed up
at the chapel right after a couple got in a fight over the
groom losing all their honeymoon money at the black-
jack table in the casino. She stormed out, and since the
minister had an open slot, so to speak, we just sort of
took it."

"So you're actually expecting me to believe that you
and the publishing world's answer to Indiana Jones—

whom you'd just met—were married in Camelot by some spell-spouting wizard?"

K.J.'s lips curved into a faint smile at the memory of the courtiers trumpeting the recessional led by harlequin-suited jugglers and tumblers. And how later, back in Alec's suite, they'd laughed about the ludicrous, but surprisingly romantic ceremony.

"I suppose you had to be there," she murmured.

"I would have been, if anyone had thought to invite me," Molly said pointedly.

"As I said, it was a spur of the moment thing."

"I guess so. Considering you were only in Las Vegas three days." Molly took another drink of wine; K.J. could practically see the wheels turning in her head. "And after you got back to Manhattan, you spent the next three days in bed. You said you must have caught something on your trip."

She'd spent those days with the blanket over her head, hiding out, trying to shut herself off from the world—or at least Alec Mackenzie's part of it—unable to decide if she wanted him to track her down or not.

When she didn't answer, Molly shot a significant look down at the unadorned finger on K.J.'s left hand. "I also would have remembered if you'd come back to Manhattan wearing a wedding ring."

K.J. fiddled nervously with the chopsticks. The memory was one of the most unpleasant of her life. Even worse than the fight they'd had. "I left it behind."

Bought in the Sir Galahad's Golden Gifts jewelry store conveniently situated just a few feet from the chapel, it had been a simple gold band, woven in an ancient Celtic pattern celebrating both their families' heritage. Although it certainly hadn't been as flashy as some of the rings displayed, K.J. had fallen in love with it at first glance. And when Alec had slipped it onto her finger she couldn't have been more thrilled if he'd gifted her with the Hope diamond.

"Sounds as if the ring wasn't the only thing you left behind. What happened, did the guy get cold feet the morning after?"

"No. In fact, he was amazingly cheerful." At least in the beginning.

"I may never have walked down the aisle, but I believe it's natural for the groom to be in a good mood the morning after his wedding night."

"It wasn't exactly your normal wedding night."

"Oh, lord." Molly frowned. "Please don't tell me Alec Mackenzie is into some sort of kinky sex."

"Of course he wasn't." The sex hadn't been kinky, although it had been amazingly inventive. He'd done things to her that no man had ever done before; encouraged her to do things to him she'd never done. And as the long, love-filled night passed, K.J. had discovered exactly how passionate she could be.

She sighed as the memories of his strong dark fingers playing on her hot moist skin set her body to humming. "I'd never met anyone like Alec," she said, trying to explain what she still couldn't fully understand herself. "I'd never felt that way about another man."

It had been as if Fourth of July firecrackers had been set off inside her, while the entire Mormon Tabernacle Choir began belting out the "Hallelujah Chorus." "Which is why, I suppose, when he suggested we get married, I agreed."

And had regretted it in the bright light of a new desert day. The strange thing was that whenever she thought about those whirlwind twelve hours, K.J.

found herself regretting her impulsive actions the morning after more than the rash marriage.

"The next morning I was the one who got cold feet." She went on to explain the battle royal over Alec's mistaken belief that she'd just abandon her career and go traipsing off to some jungle in South America with him.

"Did you tell him you'd go when he proposed?"

"I don't know. Honestly, I don't remember it coming up."

"It would seem that a suggestion to go off into the jungle just might get a girl's attention," Molly said dryly.

"You'd think so, wouldn't you? But while we were sitting in Lancelot's Lounge and he was telling me all about the Spanish barge and the lost Inca gold, I have to admit my mind started to wander. All I could think about was going upstairs and having sex with him."

"Wow." Molly let out a long breath, then leaned back in her black lacquered chair and stared across the table at her long-time friend. "So, I take it you two got a quickie divorce after you got back to New York?"

"Not exactly." K.J. pretended sudden interest in the mural of the Forbidden City painted on the far wall.

"Not exactly?" Molly repeated, openly flabbergasted. "What does that mean? You either got a divorce or not. You can't be a little bit married, K.J. That's like being a little bit pregnant."

Pregnant. It had been the one thing she'd escaped that night. Strangely, lately, whenever she saw young mothers at the mall, pushing their babies in strollers, or playing with their toddlers in the park across the street from her apartment, K.J. found herself almost wishing she had gotten pregnant with Alec's child that night. Then, at least, she'd have more than these achingly bittersweet memories.

"So," Molly said, her voice breaking into K.J.'s thoughts, "you were explaining why you and the hunk aren't divorced."

"I never quite got around to it," K.J. mumbled, growing increasingly uncomfortable.

"What?" When Molly's voice rang out over the murmur of dinner conversation, K.J. flinched. "How on earth can you not get around to getting a divorce?" she hissed, lowering her voice and leaning over the table.

*That's exactly what I'd like to know. You've demonstrated a distressingly fanciful bent before, Katherine Jeanne. But this takes the cake.*

It was not the first time the voice had chided her about her still-married state. As she'd done in the past, K.J. tried her best to ignore it.

"In the beginning, I didn't know where Alec was." She resumed fiddling with her chopsticks, switching them from hand to hand.

"I thought he told you he was leaving that day for South America to search for some Spanish treasure barge."

"South America is a big continent. Obviously, I hadn't been paying enough attention as it was. I certainly didn't catch the specifics."

"I read about that upcoming trip in the back of his latest book, *The Secrets of the Maria Isabella,*" Molly said with a nod. "It sounded really exciting. Although it would have to be something special to outdo the sunken shipwreck. That was his best story so far. All that fact-based stuff about diving beneath the sea, and swimming through the captain and crew's quarters, reminded me a little of the movie *Titanic*. In fact, I stayed up all last Saturday night to finish it and..."

Her voice drifted off as her eyes widened. "Oh my God. You're the woman he dedicated it to. The lady in red. The one who changed his life."

"I'm not sure. Although I remember him saying he'd just turned that manuscript in, so he probably would have had time to add a dedication."

Although K.J. assured him it wasn't necessary, Alec had insisted on buying her a wedding dress in Guinevere's Closet, a ridiculously pricy hotel boutique. When she would have chosen a lovely cream silk, calf-length dress with a lace yoke and cuffs that seemed appropriate for a wedding, he'd immediately dismissed it as boring, plucked a scarlet-as-sin halter gown from the rack and insisted she try it on.

"Then again," she murmured now, "a man like Alec would undoubtedly know a great many women in red dresses."

"If that sexy publicity shot on the back of his books is anything to go by, that's more than likely," Molly agreed. "The thing I'm having difficulty with is seeing you in a red dress."

K.J.'s lips curved into a reluctant, reminiscent smile. "Believe it or not, I was magnificent."

She could still recall in heartbreaking detail exactly how the gown had skimmed her body like a silk caress, how she'd felt as she'd stared at her reflection in that gilt-framed dressing room mirror. The woman looking back at her had been part twin, part stranger.

Her cheeks had been flushed nearly as bright as the scarlet dress, her blue eyes had glittered with sensual feminine intent, and although she'd always thought herself too lanky to be sexy, the bias cut of the dress had revealed curves she'd never known she had. And rather than clash with her hair, as she would have suspected, the bright color had made her look like a flame from head to toe.

She'd looked, K.J. recalled, exactly like the kind of sexy, throw-caution-to-the-winds type of woman who'd elope with a man she'd only just met.

Unfortunately, when she'd awakened in Alec's arms the next morning, the sexy daredevil stranger had disappeared, leaving behind that familiar woman with generations of Scots Calvinist blood flowing in her veins. And, unfortunately, her father's fiery temper, which she'd thought she'd learned to control under her grandmother's strict tutelage.

"Wow," Molly said again. She took another bite of her Kung Pao shrimp and considered this remarkable development. "Uh-oh."

"What?"

"If you've never gotten a divorce, and Alec hasn't either... He hasn't, has he?"

"Not that I know of." During those first few weeks after she'd run away from Las Vegas, her hasty marriage and her husband, K.J. had held her breath, waiting for him to come storming back into her life to claim her. When that hadn't happened, she'd begun expecting the official papers to be delivered to her door by some anonymous process server.

But when months went by without a single word from either Alec or his attorneys, she'd reluctantly decided that he simply wasn't going to let a little detail like marriage interfere with his swashbuckling lifestyle.

"So, the guy's still technically married," Molly said.

"As far as I know." As Molly's words sank in, K.J. groaned, put her elbows onto the table and lowered her throbbing head into her hands. "Oh no. He's not a bachelor."

"It seems not. Since he's currently married to the fast-talking editor who, just a few hours ago, assured the powers-that-be she could get him to be sold to the highest bidder at the bachelor auction."

K.J. lifted her head and stared glumly across the table. "What am I going to do?"

"Well, I suppose the honest thing to do would be to go straight upstairs to the executive suites tomorrow morning, come clean and admit all."

"I suppose you're right." It was exactly what her grandmother would have instructed her to do, as unrelentingly moralistic as she was.

*Of course she is,* the voice piped up, right on cue.

"However, after all the enthusiasm you've managed to generate, such forthright behavior would undoubtedly tick all the powers-that-be off, big time, so that would definitely not be all that wise a career move," Molly considered. "I certainly wouldn't want to be the one to tell them that they've voted to give you the next month off work, with pay, and to spring for all your travel expenses to track down a married man."

"I wonder if they need editors in the French Foreign Legion," K.J. moaned.

"They might never have to find out. Face it, K.J., you don't even know if you can find your errant husband, let alone get him to agree to come to New York to take part in the auction. Why don't you just jump off that marriage bridge when and if you get to it?"

"Or burn it behind me," K.J. muttered. A thought flickered at the far reaches of her mind. "That's it!"

"What's it?"

"You're right, it's ridiculous that I'm still technically married—"

"I don't believe *ridiculous* was the word I used," Molly interrupted.

"Well, if you had used it, you would have been right. I suppose, on some level, I've been waiting for Alec to come charging back into my life on his white stallion and sweep me off my feet again." Amazingly, K.J. hadn't even realized her motives for not ending her marriage until she'd heard herself say the words out loud.

"Editing too many romance novels can do that to you," Molly agreed sagely.

"I'm going to find Alec," K.J. vowed. She lifted her chin. A determined glint that her ancestor Ian Campbell—who'd made the decision to bring his family to the New World back in the nineteenth century—would have recognized, scorched away the concern in her eyes.

"And when I do, I'm going to get him to agree to a divorce. And then, once he's a bachelor again, I'm going to talk him into participating in the auction."

"That's quite an agenda. Especially since you only have a month—less today—to pull it off. How long does it take to get a divorce in New York, anyway?"

"I don't know." Since she'd been unconsciously waiting for Alec to insist they resume their marriage, K.J. had never bothered looking into the matter. "But it's undoubtedly longer than I have." She frowned as she considered her options.

"But that doesn't need to prove a problem," she decided on another burst of resolve. "We had a quickie marriage. Surely we can get a quickie divorce in Mexico, or some Caribbean island that caters to such a thing. In fact, I think I saw a segment on *60 Minutes* not too long ago about the Dominican Republic becoming the newest divorce destination.''

"Good idea," Molly agreed dryly. "You and Alec Mackenzie can fly off to some tropical island, undo the deed, then while you've got the guy under the romantic influence of flower-scented trade winds, moonlit seas and piña coladas, you can seduce him into taking part in the auction.''

K.J. knew her friend was kidding. But as she pulled out her credit card to pay for her dinner, she reminded herself that the auction was for a good cause.

And besides, after the way Alec had stormed out of their hotel suite, then proceeded to ignore her all these months, the least he could do was cooperate. Especially when such cooperation would legally give him what he obviously valued most—his freedom.

# 3

By the time she arrived at the group of palm-thatched buildings in what only an extremely charitable person could call a village, K.J. had decided that if she did ever find Alec, she wasn't going to divorce him. She was going to kill him.

And then, she vowed, as she climbed out of the dangerously small dugout canoe, once she'd finished with Alec, she was going to move on to whoever it was who'd lied about natural fibers being able to breathe.

Her lovely tobacco-hued linen pantsuit, which had seemed so practical when she'd been planning this South American expedition back in Manhattan, was hopelessly wrinkled. And not stylishly rumpled, either, but sopping-wet-stick-to-your-body wrinkled.

She'd bought a wide straw hat to shade her face from the unrelenting sun at a market in the last village she'd stopped at—a trading post where she'd been stranded for two excruciatingly long days—but she could still feel the unmistakable heat of a sunburn blazing on her face. And although she'd pulled her hair into a practical ponytail, several unruly strands had escaped the elasticized band and were clinging damply to her neck.

And if all this wasn't frustrating enough, precious time was running out. It had taken her a week to track down Alec's agent, who'd been away at a European book fair.

Then it had taken nearly another five days to get all her paperwork in order—which was what she got for letting her passport expire, she'd thought glumly as she'd waited in line for the photo that made her look like an escapee from a maximum-security prison.

Even then, she'd run up against another roadblock when it had taken nearly another week to find Alec. If she couldn't get his cooperation in the next six days and return to New York with him in tow, she could not only kiss her promotion goodbye, but perhaps even her job. Which was what she got, she thought, for rashly agreeing to the plan in the first place.

Two days ago, when the rickety old bus had come to a halt and the driver, a wizened, toothless man who looked older than Methuselah, had informed her in a barely comprehensible mix of Spanish, English and some Indian language she couldn't recognize that they'd reached the end of the line, she'd feared she was destined to be permanently stuck in the middle of the jungle.

Then, blessedly, this man had shown up, informed her that he just happened to be on the way to the very village she sought, and offered her a ride down the river. K.J. had admittedly suffered trepidations when she'd gotten her first look at the dugout canoe, but reminding herself that beggars couldn't exactly be choosers, she'd gratefully accepted.

"Do you know where I could find Mr. Mackenzie?" she asked the boatman.

Her savior was short and stocky, built rather along the lines of a tree trunk, with a swarthy complexion and a droopy black mustache that added to his fierce appearance. He paused from unloading her suitcases from the canoe and glanced up at the sky, which was darkening quickly. And dangerously.

K.J. had already learned the hard way that this was the rainy season; every afternoon, black anvil-shaped thunderclouds would build up, then dump an amazing amount of rain on the already soaked and flooded river basin.

"This time of day, Señor Mackenzie will be in the cantina."

She glanced around the village of Santa Clara, studying it more carefully than she had when the man had first paddled the boat up to the bank. Sober-faced men, clad in little more than bark-cloth skirts and fetish necklaces made of bright feathers and animal teeth, honed the blades of steel machetes, while women bent over cooking fires and naked children painted each other with bright dyes.

The scene was crying out to be saved on film. Momentarily putting aside her exhaustion, and her ongoing frustration at the trials of tracking down her husband, K.J. lifted her compact 35 mm camera and snapped off a roll of rapid-fire shots, including what she knew would be the highlight of the group—one of a mahogany-hued little girl who'd tethered a magnificent butterfly nearly the size of one of her hands to a thread and was flying it over her head like a bright blue kite.

The boatman, who apparently had grown accustomed to the crazy lady and her ever-present camera, watched disinterestedly, waiting for her to finish.

The buildings, as seen through her viewfinder, appeared to be a hodgepodge of scraps of tree limbs, thatching and mud. Unfortunately, despite their admittedly photogenic appeal, none of them looked all that inviting.

"Which of the buildings is the cantina?"

"It is at the far edge of the village." The way this trip

had gone thus far, K.J. wasn't at all surprised when he pointed toward the most dilapidated shanty of the bunch. Terrific.

Reminding herself that if she pulled this mission off, the exotic photographs she'd already taken on this trip might just buy her freedom from her nine-to-five routine, K.J. stiffened her aching back. And her resolve.

*"Gracias."* K.J. reached into her canvas tote bag, pulled out some of the colorful bills she'd changed her American money into when she'd first landed in the country, and managed to find, deep inside her, a reasonably friendly smile.

"Could you please take my bags to the hotel?" She pronounced it the way her three-day speed Spanish and Portuguese language course had taught her, dropping the *h.*

When he just looked at her, K.J. pulled out the pocket-size Berlitz language guide and began leafing through the pages. *"El refugio,"* she said, trying the Spanish word the book assured her was used to describe a small inn in a remote region. In K.J.'s mind, it would have been impossible to get more remote than this.

He merely shook his head, his expression suggesting that only a crazy American would be foolish enough to expect any type of accommodations in this primitive outback. She tried again, making the slight verbal shift to Portuguese. Then, thinking perhaps he was having trouble with the word *bags,* she tried several that seemed to refer to suitcases. Still nothing.

All right. She could handle this, K.J. assured herself. The same way she'd handled every other horrendous thing that had happened to her since she'd first stepped off that plane into this steaming sauna the natives insisted on calling a country. The first order of the day was obviously to find someplace to stay.

"Do tourists ever come here? *Turistas?*"

"Oh, *sí.*" His teeth flashed beneath the drooping mustache and he nodded his head vigorously. "Many *turistas.*"

Now they were getting somewhere, she thought with a burst of optimism she hadn't felt for days. "*Bien. A donde...*" her exhausted mind went blank "...do they stay?" she finished in English.

"At the lodge. It is *nuevo*. New," he translated. "It was built with a grant Señor Santos got us from the government."

Although she had no idea who Señor Santos was, relief flooded over K.J. in a cooling wave, washing away her pessimism. A lodge! And one that had been built recently! She could not have been more thrilled if he'd informed her that Windsor Castle had been air-freighted to this jungle outpost.

"Well, then, the lodge sounds *muy bien,*" she said, like him, continuing to utilize a mixture of English and Spanish. Deciding that things were definitely looking up, she bestowed her most dazzling, appreciative smile upon him. "Could you take my bags there while I meet with Mr. Mackenzie, *por favor?*"

"*Lo siento, señora.*" He shook his dark head. "I cannot do that."

A frustration that was becoming all too familiar flared like a bonfire in her gut. K.J. managed, just barely, to control it. As well as her temper.

"Why not? If it's a question of money—"

"Oh, no, *señora.*" If the boatman was at all intimidated by her tone, he certainly hid it well. K.J. also fleetingly wondered how he knew she was married, but concerned about where she was going to spend the night, she didn't dwell on that question very long. "The lodge is sold out. For the festival," he explained helpfully.

Since she couldn't care less, other than that it seemed to be keeping her from locating a bed for the night, K.J. didn't ask what festival.

She huffed a frustrated breath, realizing that she was undoubtedly coming close to the ugly American stereotype, but exhaustion and frustration, laced with a rising desperation, had begun to whittle away her social graces.

"Well, I certainly can't return to the trading settlement now that I've come all this way." K.J. feared it might sound as if she were whining. At this point, she also didn't much care. "Especially with the rains about to begin."

When planning this spur-of-the-moment trip, K.J. had failed to factor in the monsoon season.

Growing increasingly cranky, she splayed her hands on her hips and exhaled another frustrated breath. "So, do you have any suggestions where I might be able to sleep tonight?"

"*Lo siento.*" He didn't look all that sorry, K.J. thought suspiciously. In fact, he seemed to be enjoying himself immensely at the expense of the foolish American *señora.* "I do not know." His expression brightened. "You ask Señor Mackenzie. He will tell you what to do."

"Thank you." She figured that after their battle, Alec might have a few choice words on exactly what she could do. Unfortunately, in her view, there was more than enough blame to go around. They'd both made mistakes. Now it was time to remedy them and get on with their individual lives.

She looked at the three canvas suitcases, which had

turned out to be about two and a half more than she'd needed for this excursion. She'd discovered the first day that the hair dryer was definitely overkill, since there wasn't any place to plug it in out in the jungle. And when her makeup had melted off her face within the first hour, she'd given up even trying to wear anything but sunscreen.

"Will my bags be safe if I just leave them here until I talk with Señor Mackenzie?"

Openly affronted, the boatman pulled himself up to his full height of approximately five foot four and gave her something just short of a glare. "There are no thieves in this village," he informed her with the haughtiness of an ancient Inca king. "Except, perhaps, among the white *Norteamericanos* who come here for the festival."

Well, she'd certainly been put in her place, K.J. thought with a sigh.

She'd truly hoped that when the boatman had miraculously shown up at her darkest moment, informing her that he was headed home to the very village she'd been told Alec was staying in, that his appearance was an omen. A portent that her luck—which had been miserable for the week she'd been on this wild-goose chase—was about to change. Unfortunately, it seemed she'd been wildly optimistic.

"*Lo siento*," she said contritely, using his language to emphasize her regret. "I truly didn't mean to insult you. Or your neighbors."

She took out a disintegrating tissue and wiped at the moisture that continued to pearl on her forehead. "It's just that this has been a very long and trying trip and I'm afraid my patience is beginning to wear thin." She figured that bit of English would undoubtedly be way over his head.

"You do not concern yourself, *señora*." His teeth flashed assurance in his square dark face. "You ask Señor Mackenzie. He will fix things right."

"One can only hope," she murmured.

She paused, eyeing the cantina across the village square with very real trepidation. Then, bolstering up her flagging courage, and hooking the strap of her camera bag over her shoulder, she waded into the breach.

"SHE'S ARRIVED."

Alec glanced up at Rafael. "It's about time. Men have gotten to the moon in less time than it took her to reach us."

"She has not had an easy time of it."

"No."

Alec had known that the trip would provide a great deal of culture shock, but even he couldn't have predicted Kate's continual run of rotten luck. He'd been keeping track of her since her arrival in the country; when it had appeared that she was actually going to end up stranded at that trading post upriver, he'd sent one of his men to fetch her.

"And I have a feeling it's not going to get a great deal easier."

His long-time friend eyed him with interest. "I didn't realize you held such a deep grudge."

Irritated by the way her arrival had him feeling unreasonably nervous, Alec took a long drink of beer. "I'm a Scots Highlander." Indeed, Fionn Loch, one of the most remote and isolated areas in the Gaelic land of Gairloch, in what was now the British Isles, had been ruled by his ancestors for generations. "We're warriors. Holding grudges is a national pastime."

"You're third-generation American," Rafael countered. "It's been a very long time since your clansmen have put on their tartans and followed a piper into battle."

"True." Alec had always considered it a shame that he'd missed that era of clans and all-powerful lairds and raids. It might have been deadly, but at least a man wouldn't have been bored. "But it's in the blood." He shrugged. "Who am I to fight nature?"

"Who indeed?" Rafael agreed. "After all, it is something in my blood that brought me back to my own homeland when I could have become rich and famous practicing environmental law in your country.... Ah, it appears your wife has found you," he murmured as the door opened, filling the cantina with a flood of light. "And now I finally understand why you are so obsessed with the woman."

At any other time, Alec would have argued the use of the word *obsessed*, even though, in truth, he'd have to admit that it fit. But at the moment, as his palms went sweaty, all he could do was stare at the vision backlit by the soft, shimmering afternoon light.

She'd paused in the open doorway, as if waiting for her eyes to adjust to the interior darkness, giving Alec an opportunity to study her undetected.

Her red hair, a rich vibrant shade somewhere between a Highland sunset and the flames of an ancient pagan fire, was hidden beneath a wide-brimmed straw hat he recognized as native made. But escaped tendrils clung wetly to a long lissome neck that on that long-ago night had smelled of Ivory soap. Her normally creamy complexion was lobster red, evidence that the hat hadn't entirely kept the sun off her face.

Her body, beneath a very unsexy and drab pantsuit, appeared even more slender than that night he'd bought her the red wedding dress. The damp trousers clung to her legs.

She looked hot, sweaty, exhausted, cranky, and downright wrung out. But she was still the most beautiful woman he'd ever seen. And from the expressions on the faces of the other men in the cantina, Alec suspected he wasn't alone.

"Good luck, my friend," Rafael murmured as he drifted away from the table, apparently choosing to view the reunion from a safe distance away at the bar.

Alec barely noticed his departure. Instead, his attention remained riveted to the doorway. When his breath caught in his lungs in a way that was all too familiar, it took him a painful minute to remember how to breathe.

Annoyed by the surge of sensual hunger her appearance invoked, he didn't rise to greet her. Refusing to give her the upper hand, he merely lifted the dark brown bottle in a laconic salute that was at odds with his white-knuckled fingers.

"Well, Mrs. Mackenzie. Fancy meeting you all the way out here in the middle of nowhere."

For a woman who'd shown a great deal of determination and fortitude while tracking her husband all the way to this back-of-beyond settlement, Kate sure as hell didn't seem all that eager to see him. In fact, he couldn't help noticing the way she flinched at his use of her married name. Tough.

As angry as he still was at her, Alec couldn't help admiring the way she stiffened her spine, then crossed the room to the table.

"Dr. Livingstone, I presume?" she asked. Her cool tone was laced with a sarcasm that only made Alec more determined not to go easy on her.

"Cute, darlin'," he drawled. Leaning back in the

chair, he linked his fingers behind his head and flicked a bland gaze from her head to her toes, then back up to her eyes. "And, I suppose, reasonably appropriate under the circumstances. So, to what do I owe this visit?"

Unwilling to surrender the upper hand, she shrugged nonchalantly. "I've been working horrendous hours lately. I figured it was time for a vacation."

"And all the Caribbean resorts were sold out?"

Another shrug. "The Caribbean has been overdone. I was looking for new frontiers." Quickly tiring of the game, she took a deep breath and shoved at some damp curls that had fallen across her eye. "Actually, I was looking for you."

"I figured that might be the case. So, how did you find me?" he asked with an outward lack of interest.

"Your agent told me where you were. And that you were still searching for your barge of gold."

She was holding her camera bag in front of her like a talisman. Or, Alec considered, a shield. She'd taken off her dark glasses upon entering the bar, allowing him to view those wide, thickly lashed eyes that were as blue as her blood. And at the moment, guarded.

"It's proven more elusive than I'd hoped," he admitted. "However, since I'm a stickler for protecting my privacy, I'm surprised she told you where to find me."

That was a flat-out lie. He'd given both his agent and editor instructions that if Katherine Jeanne Campbell was to ever break down and call, she was to be told where he was. Then he was to be notified immediately.

"I can be very persuasive when I put my mind to it," she said.

"I remember." His smile was slow, wicked and designed to bring back sensual memories of all the hot, sexy things she'd begged him to do to her. With her.

The way she honestly looked dead on her feet began to strum reluctant sympathetic chords, so he stood and pulled a bamboo chair up to the table, positioning her across from him. "You've come a long way. Why don't you sit down and I'll order you a beer?"

"I don't drink beer." She did, however sink down onto the chair with a grateful sigh. "Although I think I'd kill for a glass of water." How was it, K.J. wondered, that her mouth could have suddenly gone so dry when the jungle air had to be made up of at least ninety percent moisture?

"Your call. Although I have to warn you, sweetheart, you'll be up half the night regretting it."

He watched understanding dawn in her exhausted eyes. Eyes that were clownishly white-rimmed from having been protected from the sun's brutal rays by her dark glasses. The smudges of purple shadows beneath those white circles revealed a recent lack of sleep.

Alec had always been able to sleep anywhere at anytime—indeed, his work demanded such talent. Yet he could understand how this alien environment—the nighttime roar of jaguars and the almost human cries of howler monkeys—could keep a newcomer awake.

"Oh. Of course. I should have thought of that." When she absently rubbed her temples, he noticed the unadorned ring finger on her left hand and experienced another surge of the icy fury he was determined to keep to himself. "I brought my own bottled water," she said, "like the tour books suggested, but my last two are in my suitcase, back at the dock."

She absently bit her pouty bottom lip as she considered her options. Alec was irritated when he found the sight outrageously sexy and more than a little appealing. Her weary gaze shifted toward the rustic bar, where Sonia was doing a halfhearted job of washing glasses. The barmaid was pretending not to look at them, but Alec suspected those dark eyes weren't missing a thing.

"I'd kill for a Diet Pepsi. But I don't suppose this place serves soft drinks."

"Not in this lifetime."

In an obvious gesture of frustration, K.J. pulled off the straw hat, tugged the elastic band loose and dragged her fingers through her tangled mass of damp, bright auburn hair. "Then it appears I don't have much choice."

He shrugged his shoulders. "We always have choices, Kate."

Alec remembered how she'd informed him that first night that she never allowed anyone to call her Kate. In turn, he'd assured that he wasn't just anyone. Later, in bed, she'd been too diverted by other things to protest.

She might have been visibly exhausted and appear as if her last nerve was on the verge of unraveling, but the way she suddenly thrust out that foxy little chin reminded Alec of how she'd looked when she'd informed him that she had no intention of traipsing off to some godforsaken jungle with him in search of buried treasure.

"You're enjoying this, aren't you?"

"Me?" He wanted to throttle her. He wanted to touch her. Alec managed to resist both and instead put a hand against his chest in a gesture of innocence. "Why would I be enjoying seeing my bride look so miserable?"

He almost felt sorry for her when she flinched again. Almost. "I'm not your bride."

"Point taken. Technically, I suppose after all these months we might be considered out of our honeymoon stage. If we'd had a honeymoon," he added. "So, I stand corrected. You're not my bride. You're my wife."

She was biting that sexy bottom lip again in a way that, even as his irritation was soaring, made him want to soothe the red mark away with his tongue. Which left him feeling even more angry. At himself and at her.

"Not really."

"That's funny. I happen to have a paper saying you are."

He was now furious enough that if he'd been Angus Mackenzie, laird of the clan Mackenzie back in the 1500s, he wouldn't have hesitated to haul her over his lap and apply a few smacks to that firm little butt. Civilization being what it was, Alec reluctantly decided he'd have to find some other way to discipline his bride.

"And in case you weren't paying attention when you signed our marriage license, no one penciled in a provision for alternate interpretations to that man-and-wife-till-death-us-do-part clause of the contract," he reminded her.

"Don't do this, Alec." He watched, unreasonably fascinated, as her remarkable eyes went from fire to frost. He knew, without any doubt, that he could melt that ice before she could open her mouth to protest. "We both know that our marriage was a mistake."

Her firmly set lips were practically daring him to kiss them into pliancy. Once again, Alec resisted temptation as he arched a laconic brow.

"Speak for yourself, darling."

Although he'd tried to tell himself these past months that he was getting over Kate, just looking at her, having her so physically close but emotionally so far away, hurt like hell. Her betrayal ripped at him, as sharp and lethal as it had that morning.

"As a Campbell yourself, Kate, you should know that back home in the Highlands, a man's word was always his bond. Hell, it probably still is, for that matter. The Mackenzies have always prided themselves on honoring their vows, and since I don't plan on dying anytime soon, and you appear in fine fettle, albeit a bit road weary right now—" he skimmed a glance over her "—it appears, Mrs. MacKenzie, as if you're stuck."

# 4

K.J.'s MIND WAS WHIRLING. All this time in the jungle must have gotten to him, because Alec was obviously demented. And even if he wasn't mad, he was definitely dangerous. The man facing her across the wobbly table might live in the twentieth century, but he was unmistakably a warrior of old. His cheekbones were a ruthless slash, his square jaw was firmly set and his eyes were case-hardened steel.

She had no trouble picturing him living back during those brutal times of Highland clans, warring, pillaging, raping. Not that he'd ever have to rape any woman, she thought as hormones that seemed to have gone into hibernation after she'd escaped Las Vegas sudden awakened and began bouncing around inside her like steel balls in a pinball machine.

She had to focus on why she'd come all this way to the middle of the Amazon jungle. It was imperative that she keep her mind on her goal and her eyes on the prize.

Fighting for calm, determined that he not sense her trepidation, she met his dangerous, unblinking gaze straight on.

"In case you haven't noticed, Alec, we're not exactly living in the seventeenth century."

"Oh, I've noticed, Kate," he drawled. "Which is why I've never held the Campbells' bloody murderous deeds against you."

"You can't be serious. That was over three centuries ago!"

Although the episode wasn't actually spoken of in her family, she could not have been of Scots heritage and not known of the country's most notorious massacre. Which was, considering its violent history, really saying something. It had been on a cold February night in 1692, when a group of soldiers from the clan Campbell, housed by the MacDonalds, rose up and murdered their hosts. According to Alec's version of the ancient tale, one of the MacDonald wives had come from the Mackenzie clan.

"Besides, the Mackenzies weren't actually saints," she insisted, not bothering to defend the indefensible.

"Ah, now we're back to the tale of Fergus Mackenzie allegedly stealing a Campbell's cattle."

"It was more than alleged. The Mackenzie was subsequently hanged for his crimes."

"Since the Campbells had sold out to the English king, it's not surprising the law ruled the way it did," he retorted.

"And am I to assume that you'd also be blaming the English for your ancestor Mackenzie stealing away a Campbell wife?"

"Only because the Campbell was known throughout Scotland for getting drunk and beating the poor woman. I'd do the same thing myself in a heartbeat. Although," he admitted, "if she were half as much of a trial as you, my darling Kate, I might have been tempted to beat her myself."

"You wouldn't dare."

"I wouldn't put it to the test."

How did he do it? K.J. wondered furiously. This conversation she'd thought she'd planned so well during her trip to the Amazon was turning out to be a replay of that fatal morning, when an argument over the future of their marriage had escalated into a ridiculous argument over a centuries-old blood feud that both families should have put behind them when they'd landed on American shores.

"You're doing it again," she complained. "Sidetracking me. This isn't about clans or murders, or stolen cows, or even adulterous wives, Alec. I've come to discuss a divorce."

"Have you now?" He eyed her blandly over the mouth of the bottle as he took another long drink of beer that he was suddenly wishing was something stronger. "And here I figured you'd braved those river rapids to suggest that, after all these months of separation, we should finally begin living as man and wife."

"Alec, that little speech about how the Mackenzie men always honor their vows is all very good and makes you sound incredibly noble, despite being the descendent of a convicted and hanged thief." She couldn't resist tacking that on. "But surely you can't expect it to apply in this case."

"I don't see why not. Just because times change doesn't mean that morals and honor should be tossed aside. Perhaps, if more men felt the way I do, the divorce rate wouldn't be so high."

K.J. thought of all the friends she knew who'd complained that their husbands no longer paid attention to them now that they'd married, or worse yet, the ones whose husbands had been unfaithful to their vows, and reluctantly admitted that he might have a point. But she had no intention of admitting that.

"I hadn't realized you'd earned a degree in sociology."

"I don't need a degree to know that too many

men—and women—take their marriage vows too lightly."

"Exactly." Now they were finally getting somewhere, K.J. thought. "And, like it or not, that's what happened to us, Alec. We were both swept away with the emotion of that night, neither of us knew what we were doing—"

"I knew," he interrupted quietly.

"What?" She pushed some tangled hair off her forehead with an impatient hand and stared at him.

"I knew exactly what I was doing that night."

"Oh…well, that makes one of us." She took a deep breath and forced herself not to look away from his unblinking gaze. "The thing is, I wasn't exactly myself that night and I don't think that both of us should have to keep paying for my mistake."

"But I've told you, Kate, I don't consider it a mistake. The way I see it, our only mistake was not living together afterward."

"We've already been through that."

"The hell we have." His mild voice turned to stone. Granite, she thought, covered in sleet.

His jaw clenched painfully. When frustration rose hot and acrid in his throat, Alec picked up the beer and swallowed to force it back down. When he slammed the empty bottle onto the table, their gazes locked again.

"I may be a typical man when it comes to avoiding conversations about male-female relationships, Kate, but even I don't consider a few brief lines scribbled on a piece of hotel stationery all that much of a discussion."

Once again K.J. couldn't deny that he had a very valid point. Which was the real reason why, coward that she was when it came to this man, she'd avoided even attempting to get in touch with him since that horrid morning.

Although she'd been telling herself for months that hers and Alec's marriage was not only a reckless mistake, but a sham as well, she couldn't honestly justify the way she'd chosen to escape it. She'd opted for the coward's way out. And had regretted it ever since.

"You walked out on me first," she insisted.

"I may have left the suite," he allowed, "for a time." The steel in his voice now echoed the glint in his eyes. "But I wasn't the one who walked away from our marriage."

Another good point, dammit. "I suppose, all things considered, you're entitled to an explanation," she conceded.

"On that we agree." He leaned back and folded his arms over his chest.

A chest that, heaven help her, K.J. could remember kissing on her way down to his taut stomach. And beyond. A heat that had nothing to do with the equatorial temperatures flooded into her cheeks, scorching her already sunburned skin.

"So, shoot, my dear wife," he invited. "I've been waiting a very long time to hear this excuse."

She'd had such a nice little speech prepared back in Manhattan. Clever words she'd written on her laptop computer and edited again and again to get precisely the proper repentant tone. Words designed to end their ill-conceived marriage and convince him to accompany her back to New York for Heart Books's bachelor auction. Words she'd memorized on her flight to South America, then had honed one last time on her boat ride down the river.

Unfortunately, like everything else where Alec

Mackenzie was concerned, nothing about this trip was going as planned.

She nervously cleared her parched throat.

"I fully intend to explain. But first, if you don't mind, I believe I'll take you up on that offer of a beer, after all."

When a few more damp tangles of hair fell over her eye, she pushed them back over her shoulder. "I swear it's as hot in here as it is outside."

"You know what they say. It's not the temperature, but the humidity." He lifted two fingers toward Sonia, who'd given up all pretense of work and was now openly watching them, her dark eyes revealing her obvious irritation at the appearance of a female rival. "We're smack in the middle of the monsoon season."

"So I've discovered." K.J. could feel the sweat beading unattractively above her upper lip. She took a tissue from one of the outside pockets of her camera bag and blotted it away. "What kind of rain doesn't cool things down, anyway?"

"The jungle kind. In case you haven't noticed, sweetheart, you're not exactly in Kansas anymore."

"I've never even been to Kansas." But the state famous for its sweet corn had to be a lot more hospitable than this place. K.J. found herself wishing for a pair of sparkly ruby slippers so she could click the heels together and escape this suffocating, verdant green steam bath.

"Don't be so damn literal. As an editor, you of all people should recognize a metaphor."

Exhaustion, heat and nerves tangled, making her want to scream. Or throw something. If she hadn't had her period before embarking on this ridiculously conceived adventure, K.J. might have suspected she'd come down with the world's worst case of PMS.

"And you, as such a hotshot adventure writer, should be able to come up with a more original one," she countered as she took off the wrinkled jacket and tossed it over the back of the empty chair beside her. Unfortunately, it didn't help. She didn't feel one whit cooler.

"Ah, but that's what I have an editor for," he said. "To keep me honest. And reasonably original."

As frustrated as she was, K.J. couldn't deny that he was definitely an original. She'd never met a man anything like Alec Mackenzie. And she also figured she could probably go the rest of her life without ever meeting another.

That idea caused her mood to shift quickly and dramatically. Now, instead of wanting to shout or scream at him, K.J. found herself on the verge of tears. Having never been a crybaby, she could only conclude that she must be having a nervous breakdown.

Trying to survive in a hostile jungle environment could probably cause any sane person to become a bit unraveled, she assured herself, grasping for any thin straw of reason. Which unfortunately didn't say a lot for the potential of success during the rest of her mission.

A silence settled over the table. Since she'd already admitted she hadn't come all this way to jump into his hammock and begin making up for lost time, Alec certainly wasn't in any hurry for Kate to put her cards on the table.

He was more than willing to wait her out. As he'd been doing for the past eleven-plus months. Months he'd swung back and forth between cold fury, dogged determination and atypical pessimism.

It was the pessimism he was most angry about. It had not only been highly uncharacteristic, but damn surprising. A man who traveled the world chasing after hidden treasure had to be, by nature, an optimist. But Kate's betrayal had changed all that.

And if that wasn't bad enough, always underlying everything was a deep, unrelenting, painful desire for his runaway bride that went all the way to the marrow of his bones.

Across the table, K.J. sighed again. Heavier, deeper, in a way that did intriguing things to her breasts. Alec watched the way they rose and fell beneath the sodden white T-shirt she'd worn beneath her unlined linen jacket, and felt that all-too-familiar hunger pool painfully in his loins.

He wondered what she'd do if he just threw her over his shoulder and carried her out of the cantina to his hut, where he could rip off those ugly damp clothes, bury himself deep inside her and satiate the sexual hunger he'd tried like hell to ignore but which had been clawing at him since he'd first heard she was on her way to his jungle outpost. It was certainly what his Mackenzie ancestors would have done.

Sometimes, Alec concluded grimly, civilization sucked.

The thick, uneasy mood was momentarily shattered by Sonia's arrival at the table. The ebony-haired barmaid slammed the bottles down, causing foam to bubble over the top and down the sides of the brown glass. Her expression worlds away from her usual bold, flirtatious one, she snatched the colorful bills from Alec's hand, shoved them into the front of her embroidered cotton blouse, speared a hot lethal glare at K.J., then stomped away.

"I do hope I'm not interfering with anything personal," K.J. murmured, watching the way the barmaid's skirt rustled with the exaggerated sway of her voluptuous hips.

K.J. wondered if the woman had been serving Alec more than just beer, and was surprised when that thought made her want to tear that thick black hair out by the roots. And that was just for starters.

"Nothing worth mentioning." Alec decided that Kate's unsuccessful attempt to keep the jealousy from her voice was encouraging. He might not be an expert on marriage, but he suspected that a jealous wife was not an indifferent one.

Because he could no longer be this close to his runaway wife without touching her, he skimmed a fingertip down the back of the hand that was resting on the table. She was still wearing her nails unpolished, and even though they were as short as they'd been when he'd slipped that woven gold ring on her finger, Alec could remember, in vivid detail, exactly how they'd felt digging into his shoulders, raking down his bare back, holding on for dear life as he'd taken them beyond the dangerous rapids into the raging torrent.

"Would it bother you if you were?"

"Were what?" she asked softly, seeming entranced by the sight of his dark fingers on her skin.

"Interfering in some hot illicit affair I was having with Sonia?" He was honestly interested, then equally annoyed when he realized he was practically holding his breath, awaiting her answer.

"Not at all."

Sonia. Even the woman's name sounded lush and sexy, K.J. thought grimly. A woman named Sonia would never wear taupe career-woman suits, worry about E-mail or deadlines. A woman named Sonia would be too busy with hot, hedonistic pleasures to get anywhere near a slush pile.

"What you do—and with whom you do it—is entirely your business." Liar. Heaven help her, she did care, K.J. realized with surprise. Too much.

Alec might have almost believed her had it not been for the faint, almost indiscernible tremor in her voice.

"I never realized you were one of those modern women who believe in open marriages."

"Of course I don't. I've always been a firm believer in monogamy. However, despite your insistence that we have a contractual obligation, Alec, you can't deny that no court in the land could possibly uphold a contract that was entered into with false intentions."

"Sorry," he said, perversely enjoying being difficult. After all, she'd certainly put him through enough grief. Until Katherine Jeanne Campbell had come crashing into his life, Alec hadn't even realized that one woman—and a skinny one at that—could possess the power to take over his mind and body and make him so damn miserable. "But I, for one, wasn't the one with false intentions. In fact, I was up front with you from the very beginning. Other guys might have just been satisfied with a one-night stand. But I explained that I wanted more than that from you, Kate. A lot more."

Since K.J. couldn't quite figure out how to admit she hadn't been really listening all that closely to what he'd been saying that night, she didn't reply.

Alec turned his hand, linking their fingers together. "My parents met when they were undergraduates at Cornell," he said quietly. "They were divorced when I was nine, which didn't really bother me, since I was in boarding school at the time and never saw them all that much, anyway.

"My mother went on to have a successful career as a concert pianist and acquired two more husbands before I graduated from college. The last time I heard from my father, who's an anthropologist, he was somewhere in New Zealand, studying aborigines and about to take a fourth wife. She's the daughter of some tribal chief. She's also one-third his age."

She might have missed a few pertinent bits of information that night, but K.J. knew she'd remember him telling her all this.

"That must have been difficult," she murmured, her heart aching for the boy he must have been. At least she'd shared nine wonderful, exciting years with her globe-trotting parents.

"It wasn't as bad as it probably sounds to an outsider. Their careers were the main focus of their lives, and they were both incredibly selfish people. I was merely a mistake from a drunken New Year's Eve."

"They actually told you that?" K.J. was aghast.

"Sure." Alec shrugged. The knowledge had years ago lost its ability to cause pain. "It was their explanation why they didn't have any time or room for a kid in their lives."

"I still can't imagine telling your own child that he was unwanted."

"Not exactly unwanted. They were also quick to point out that my mother didn't have to put her career on hold for those months to carry me, since she could have gotten a legal abortion in Europe. Or even by one of their medical doctor friends."

"Well, I certainly think she deserves a medal for that act of martyrdom," K.J. said dryly. "It's too bad I'm not Catholic. I could write to the Pope and nominate her for sainthood."

Alec looked at her for a long moment. "I wasn't aware you'd care."

"How could I not?" Surely he didn't think she was that cold and unfeeling?

He gave her another long look, then shrugged. "Like I said, it wasn't that bad. Since they were never around, I didn't miss them when I got sent off to that military school in New Mexico right after my sixth birthday. And from the gossip I've heard over the years, I think I lucked out not meeting some of the stepparents."

K.J. felt the moisture swimming in her eyes. "I'm sorry."

"I didn't tell you about my folks to gain sympathy, Kate. I told you so you'll understand where I'm coming from. Although I prefer to believe that we chart our own paths in life, I've also read enough pop psychology to figure my parents' problem with commitment is undoubtedly partly why I always swore that if I ever got married, it'd be for keeps.

"I never wanted any kid of mine to go to bed at night without knowing that he could call his dad to chase away any monsters that might be lurking beneath the bed or in the closet."

"We don't have a child." She didn't admit that she'd thought about one too much these past months.

"That's beside the point." He lifted their joined hands and kissed her fingertips. "We said our vows before God and Merlin. Which means that like it or not, Kate, you're my lawfully wedded wife."

"But—"

"For better or worse. And all that jazz," he added gruffly cutting off her attempted argument. The way he'd squared his broad shoulders reminded K.J. of a warrior getting ready to go into battle. Equally daunting was his gaze, which had turned as granite hard as his jaw. "So deal with it."

# 5

DRAGGING HER EYES from his penetrating gaze, pulling free of his scintillating touch, K.J. scooped up her own bottle. She lifted it to her lips and took a deep, thirsty swallow. Then immediately began to choke.

Alec was on his feet in a flash, coming around to stand behind her, slapping her on her back. "I probably should have warned you it was warm."

"That—would have been—" she forced the words out between coughs "—helpful."

"Guess I forgot." His tone said just the opposite. When her racking coughs subsided, Alec didn't take his hands away. Instead, he slid them up her back to her shoulders and began kneading the rigid stiffness.

"Surely you don't really expect me to believe that?" she said testily, batting at his hands. Alec ignored her.

"I've never known what to expect from you, Kate." Tied up in a painful knot of frustration, desire and, dammit, affection, he slipped his fingers beneath her hair and lightly squeezed the nape of her lithe neck. "Except for that first time I saw you and knew that there was one helluva lot of heat beneath that controlled, icy, New York career woman facade. And how, once I got it melted, we'd be perfect together."

His fingertips skimmed a sensual trail to that sensitive spot behind her ear that he'd learned had a direct connection to other, more vital body parts. "Which, as you'll recall, we were."

"Alec." His name was part protest, part plea. "Please. Don't do this."

"Dammit, Kate," he complained, "you can't just show up on my doorstep after all these months and expect me to behave as if that night—and our marriage—never happened."

"When you put it that way, I have to admit that it sounds a little unreasonable."

"How about a lot?" He bent his head and began nibbling at her neck, amazed to discover that the clean fresh smell of Ivory soap was actually lurking beneath the more pungent scents of Cutter insect repellent and sunscreen.

"But it still isn't as if what we've had the past eleven and a half months is anywhere near a normal marriage," she said.

"Normal's boring." His teeth closed on her earlobe. "And it definitely doesn't describe you." He moved to the other earlobe and tugged. "Or me." His tongue soothed the pink imprint left by his teeth. "Or us, together."

K.J. shifted, breaking contact. "You're right about there being a great many things we have to talk about, Alec. Things that need to be settled."

Her fingers curled around the long brown neck of the bottle so tightly that this time it was her knuckles that turned white. Growing more thirsty by the minute, whether from nerves or dehydration, she took a more careful drink.

"But I'm really not up to an in-depth discussion of our relationship right now. I've had an incredibly horrendous past few days—"

"Your choice," he noted. "Since I don't remember inviting you here."

"Actually, you did." She met his challenging gaze

with a level one of her own. "That next morning. Although it wasn't exactly an invitation," she reminded him archly. "More of an order." This time she took a longer drink, finding the wetness more than made up for the malt taste.

"I'm sorry if I took your willingness to stand by your man for granted." Alec's jaw clenched. After all this time, he still couldn't quite contain his rage at the memory of her refusal.

During these months of separation, Alec had had lots of time to think about Kate. Plenty of long lonely nights spent staring unseeingly at ancient maps and wondering about might-have-beens.

She'd seemed so damn enthusiastic about his work before their marriage. He could still remember the way she'd looked deep into his eyes, hanging on to every word he'd said, as if he'd possessed all the secrets of the universe.

He'd assumed that she'd be leaving for the jungle with him in the morning. She'd certainly not objected when he suggested the idea. Since love had had him feeling exceptionally generous, he'd even granted her time to go back to New York and hand her work over to some other editor at that romance novel publishing house.

"Besides," he growled, "you agreed to come with me while we were still sitting in Lancelot's Lounge."

"That night I would have agreed to anything." Remembering all too vividly how she'd felt, K.J. knew that Alec could have informed her that he'd been planning to fly to the moon on gossamer wings and she would have blissfully assured him that was her favorite thing to do.

"And did," he reminded her softly, his voice dropping wickedly into its lowest registers, the deep baritone designed to remind her of every hot, sexy thing they'd done together. "In fact, I remember, just before dawn, when you practically begged me to—"

"I don't need a play-by-play, Alec," K.J. insisted. "I just need a divorce."

"So you said." He rubbed his jaw and studied her, realizing that in some peripheral way, he was somewhat responsible for those dark shadows beneath her eyes. Too bad. "But since I'm not exactly feeling in a real generous mood toward you right now, Kate, I have to tell you, I'm not real inclined to give you one."

"I could file without your agreement."

"You could—and hope to hell I wouldn't contest it." He took another long pull on the beer bottle. "Then again, I suppose, if you talked real sweet, we might be able to work out a compromise."

How could she not see that the world she'd chosen for herself was so against her nature? he thought. K.J. Campbell might wear business suits that hid her curves, eat yogurt at her desk and drink coffee all day while she tried to work with a phone to her ear. He had no doubt that, as intelligent as she was, she was a hotshot editor. This trip also proved that she had one helluva lot of determination. Enough that, if she kept running along that fast track, she'd end up in the top echelons of publishing. Where she'd only be miserable.

She was a woman born to adventure. He knew enough about her famous father to know that she couldn't deny her heritage. George Campbell would not have wanted his daughter to spend her days under fluorescent lights that gave a city pallor to her creamy complexion.

He knew she'd inherited her father's unique eye for seeing the world in a special light. The question, Alec considered, was whether she'd be able to see herself as clearly as she could see what she'd captured so well through the lens of her camera: little girls with beaded hair bouncing as they jumped rope in a playground strewn with broken glass; a sunshine yellow flower valiantly forcing its way through a crack in a side-walk; old men in vested suits playing chess in the park; and a trio of helium-filled balloons rising high among the canyons of the city, bright red, yellow, and purple proof that escape was, indeed, possible.

He wondered if, once she realized her own needs, she'd be brave enough to act on them.

She was eyeing him with open suspicion. "What kind of compromise?"

"I don't know," he said mildly, ignoring the barb-wire ball of need twisting painfully in his gut. "I'll have to give it some thought. After all, there's no hurry."

As an unpalatable thought suddenly occurred to him, Alec shot a quick look down at her stomach, which beneath the pleated linen trousers seemed, if anything, almost concave due to the weight she'd lost.

Still, he reached across the table, caught her chin in his fingers and firmly held her now-wary gaze. "Is there?"

Her slight hesitation spoke volumes. Fury and jeal-ousy ripped through him like a buzz saw as he watched the movement of muscles in her throat as she swallowed.

"Is there what?"

"Any hurry?"

"No." She bit her bottom lip as her gaze shifted to somewhere beyond his left shoulder. "Not really."

She was a liar, he decided. But an exceptionally lovely one, even with her glistening, sunburned face, wild mass of red hair and that amazingly ugly and wrinkled suit.

He wondered yet again exactly what had triggered this sudden trip to the Amazon. Surely, if all she'd wanted was a divorce, she could have filed in New York and had her attorney send the papers to his agent to forward.

He wondered if there was another man in Kate's life now. Some staid, bookish fellow with round, wire-rimmed glasses, a tweed sport coat, cashmere vest and argyle socks. A man who'd never put demands on her. In bed or out.

The way Alec saw it, if she did finally get around to admitting that another man had been the impetus for this visit, he had two choices. He could fly back to the States and kill the guy with his bare hands. Or he could take advantage of her surprise appearance in Santa Clara, seduce her into his bed and scorch any would-be rivals out of her mind.

His Scots-warrior blood was burning for the first option. Reminding himself that she was right—that times, regretfully, had changed—and deciding that murderers, even those who committed crimes of passion, probably didn't get all that many conjugal visits in prison, Alec decided to choose option number two.

"So, can I take your denial to mean that you didn't brave mosquitoes the size of dive-bombers, piranhas and heatstroke to inform me that you're carrying another man's child?"

The color drained from her face, leaving it paper pale. "Of course not."

"Good." Satisfied that this, at least, was not a lie, he skimmed a thumb over her top lip, pleased by the way her startled eyes softened at his touch. "Because if there was another guy, I'd have no choice but to throw him out the window of your office." It was, of course, more fantasy than actual threat, but that little fact made the idea no less appealing.

Although he would have guessed it to be impossible, her complexion went even whiter beneath the fire-engine red sunburn.

"You wouldn't." K.J. searched his stony face for the truth. "You couldn't."

His thumb lazily teased a trail around her bottom lip. "I wouldn't bet the farm on that, Mrs. Mackenzie."

K.J. was as surprised by Alec's gritty threat as she'd been by his insistence that he wasn't going to release her from her wedding vows. After all, when he hadn't immediately followed her back to New York, stormed into her office and dragged her off by the hair to his cave—metaphorically speaking, of course—she'd come to the conclusion that he hadn't really cared about her. Or their marriage. At the time, with her emotions still all in a tangle, she hadn't known whether to feel relieved or disappointed.

But now, looking into hard, cold eyes that reminded her of the deadly machete the near-naked Indian had been sharpening when she'd first arrived in the village, K.J. was forced to wonder.

Could Alec, perhaps, actually love her? As she'd believed he had that magical, reckless night? Or was he merely possessive? A man who, while he might no longer want her for himself, didn't have any intention of letting any other man have her, either? With her mind leaping back and forth between all those possibilities, she took another longer drink of the beer, which was tasting better all the time.

"When I woke up that morning," she said slowly, momentarily forgetting her declaration that she didn't want to discuss their ill-fated marriage until after she'd had some rest, "I realized I'd married a man I didn't know all that well."

She ran a trembling finger up and down her bottle, gathering up little beads of moisture from the dark brown glass. "Now I'm beginning to realize that I don't know you at all."

"Don't worry." A warrior's smile slashed dangerously white in his darkly tanned face. "Things move a lot slower down here. There'll be plenty of time to catch up and hash this all out."

Because he wanted to crush his mouth to hers and drink from those wide lips that had drawn into a tight line, Alec forced himself to pull back from the quicksand trap this lovely, redheaded Campbell still represented.

"For now, we'll put aside our problems and just kick back and enjoy the festival. Then we can talk about a divorce."

"Festival?" She vaguely remembered the boatman saying something about a festival. And it being the reason there was literally no room at the lodge.

"Yeah." Alec sat back down across from her and picked up his beer. Although it wasn't cold, he hoped it would be wet enough to douse the flames of desire that had flared from ashes he was discovering had never entirely cooled. "It starts tomorrow at sundown. And although I'm not up on the specifics, apparently the ritual the tribe is going to perform dates back to Stone Age times." He glanced across the table at the camera bag she was holding on her lap. "You'd probably get some dynamite pictures."

"That is an appealing prospect." She wondered if *National Geographic* might be interested. They'd published her father's photos several times. Although her grandmother had thrown away her treasured copies, after spending years of weekends running around to tag sales, K.J. had managed to find most of the issues.

"A friend of mine who's more up on the culture than I am tells me that the high point of the festivities is a reenactment of an ancient fertility rite."

"Oh." Well, she definitely wasn't pale any longer. Alec watched the color flood into her cheeks as anxiety and reluctant curiosity warred in her incredible eyes. "So many Stone Age tribes have been discovered these past years, there have been a lot of such photographs published. Perhaps I'll just pass."

"What's wrong?" he taunted softly. "Don't tell me you're afraid to attend with your husband a ritual centered around sex?"

He had to give her credit when she lifted her foxy, argumentative chin again. "Not at all. I'm just not sure I'll be staying that long—"

"Oh yes, you will."

"You're so certain of that?"

"I'm damn certain that there isn't a man in this village who'll take you back upriver without my permission."

"Permission?" Her fingers began tapping dangerously on the scarred tabletop. "May I remind you again, in case you haven't noticed, Alec, that we're on the brink of the twenty-first century—"

"Not out here," he interrupted.

Damn. She suspected, from what she'd seen this far, that he might be right. Nevertheless, she wasn't about to just let him steamroll right over her. He may think himself some evolutionary product of a Scots warrior, but her own gene pool was awash in stiff-backed, equally stubborn women who didn't kowtow to any male. Not even their husbands.

"Point taken." Her own voice was as sharp as a

newly honed knife blade. "However, we're all products of our environment, and you and I live in modern times. There's no way you could get away with keeping me prisoner here."

"That's a harsh word, darling. And a bit of an exaggeration." His lips curved. "Why don't you just think of yourself as my honored guest?"

"Where have I heard that before?" she murmured. She did not often resort to sarcasm; unfortunately, Alec seemed to bring out the worst in her. "Ah yes, isn't that how Saddam Hussein referred to his human shields?"

"Now I'm truly wounded to the quick," Alec said, his mild tone and the bedeviling smile in his eyes saying just the opposite.

His seeming refusal to take her seriously caused her to unconsciously curl the fingers of her right hand into a tight fist. "If I wanted to leave, you couldn't stop me."

The smile faded from his sexy lips; his eyes turned hard. "I wouldn't put it to the test. Because you'd lose, big time." He glanced down at her hand. "And if you're thinking of slugging me, I've got to warn you, K.J., I'm not one of your prissy little prep-school boyfriends. I just may hit back."

K.J. didn't believe his threat. Not for a single second. What she did find frightening, however, was the way he could change from warmly amused to hard and dangerous in a blink of those riveting gray eyes.

And amazingly, he wasn't the only one capable of fast and wide mood swings. What was it about this man, she wondered distractedly, that kept her emotions in such turmoil?

"You wouldn't hit me," she said, straightening her

clenched fingers. It just happened to be the only thing she was certain about where Alec was concerned.

"You're probably right on that one."

"Of course I am. And if I really wanted to leave, right now, on my own—"

"It'll be the stupidest damn thing you've ever done. And believe me, Kate, from what I've seen so far, that's saying something."

She exhaled a frustrated breath. "Do you think I could please finish a thought here?"

He waved the beer bottle in a be-my-guest gesture.

"Thank you." She nodded, opting to be satisfied by any small concession she might win at this point. "As I was saying, if I did choose to head back upriver on my own, short of tying me up, you couldn't stop me."

"Now, there you go again," he complained with a sexy, mocking grin. "Tempting me. Because let me tell you, sweetheart, tying you up has a certain edgy, albeit kinky, appeal."

This time the flames didn't just rise in her face, but flared dangerously in other, more intimate, body parts as well, making K.J. feel as if she just might be on the verge of bursting into spontaneous combustion.

"Well, you're not going to get the chance," she said, summoning up the last tangled threads of her Campbell willpower. "Because, since I'm exhausted, I'd rather catch up on my sleep than attempt to row upstream in a rainstorm. So I believe I'll just spend the night in the village, after all."

"Good call."

"I'm ever so pleased you approve," she said with saccharine sweetness. "Which brings me to the subject of where I'm going to be staying. The boatman who brought me here—"

"Raul."

He was doing it again. Cutting off her thoughts in midstream, when it was difficult enough to try to keep them together without the continual interruptions. She arched a tawny brow. "Excuse me?"

"His name is Raul. Your boatman."

"Oh." Strange that he'd know that, K.J. mused. When he'd supposedly been in here drinking beer when she'd arrived. A niggling little suspicion stirred in the far reaches of her mind, causing her to wonder if perhaps her arrival here in the village wasn't such a surprise to Alec at all. It made sense that his agent would have informed him she was coming. Could he have actually sent someone upriver to fetch her?

"Well, anyway, he—Raul—" she stressed, earning another satisfied nod from him, "says that the hotel, or lodge, or whatever it's called, is booked solid."

"He's right. The tribe has only begun to allow outsiders to witness their secret ceremonies. Which pretty much guarantees a full house during festivals."

"But if the festival doesn't begin until tomorrow evening, surely there should be a bed at the lodge just for tonight."

"Sorry. The tourists always come in a day early. To get acclimated to their surroundings. And the weather."

She could certainly understand that. Although she also suspected it would take more than twenty-four hours to acclimatize to such an unfamiliar environment.

"But surely there must be someplace else—another village nearby, perhaps, or—"

"Well, there is a village a couple miles downriver Alec rubbed his unshaven jaw. "But it's not really that much of an option. Unless you're interested in ing the honored guest at dinner."

"That doesn't sound so bad." In her tourist guide on the flight from New York, she'd read about the generosity of many primitive Amazon tribes. Of course, the downside of that was that she'd also read about termites being a mainstay of several menus.

"I suppose that all depends," Alec said.

K.J. knew he wanted her to ask him to elaborate. She waited him out as long as possible, then finally threw up her hands.

"All right, I'll bite. Depends on what?"

He skimmed a darkly wicked glance over her. "Depends on how you'd feel about being served up as the entrée."

# 6

"ENTRÉE? Surely you don't mean... That can't be possible in this day and age.... You can't be saying that there are actually cannibals still living in this jungle?"

"Hey, don't worry your pretty head about it." She looked so distressed that if he wasn't still irritated at her, Alec might have almost regretted the lie. "So long as you don't go off on your own, you're fairly safe." He tilted his head and eyed her thoughtfully. "Of course, none of the natives in this isolated neck of the woods have ever seen anyone with your hair color. Which would make your lovely red head a nice prize to take back home on a stake to their chief. In fact, I'll bet such a gift might even win a headhunting warrior a night with the chief's daughter." He rubbed his jaw again. "Since you're such a rare find, they might decide to take you prisoner first. So they can try you out, so to speak, before boiling you over a fire."

Her eyes narrowed suspiciously. "You're lying." This was his way of getting even with her. She was sure of it.

*Sure enough to put it to the test?* the little voice inside her head challenged.

"You wound me, Kate. Is that any way for a wife to talk to her beloved husband?"

His wolfish smile had K.J. feeling a great deal like Red Riding Hood. Oh, it was unarguably charming. But, she suspected, ultimately dangerous.

Before she could challenge him further, a tall, handsome man appeared beside their table.

"Alec," he said, his liquid brown eyes focused on K.J., "aren't you going to introduce me to your lovely companion?" His voice was every bit as warm and smooth as his eyes.

Although Rafael was a close friend, Alec damn well didn't like him looking at Kate the way a starving man might look at a piece of prime rib.

"Kate, this is a friend of mine, Rafael Santos. Rafael, this is Katherine Jeanne Mackenzie. My wife," he reminded his friend, just in case he may have forgotten that salient little point.

"Hello, Señor Santos," K.J. said politely.

"*Buenos dias*, Señora Mackenzie." Alec seethed as Rafael lifted K.J.'s outstretched hand to his lips, continental style. "Welcome to our little village. It's a pleasure to meet you at last."

He was smiling as he gave her an unthreatening, but thoroughly male perusal. "Alec has told me a great deal about you, but I see now that even his effusive words regarding your charm and beauty were an understatement."

Oh, he was smooth, K.J. thought. Smooth as melted Hershey's chocolate. And despite his movie-star-handsome looks and that flattering dark gaze that would have strummed feminine chords in any woman, he didn't affect her the way Alec could without even trying.

"That's very flattering, Señor Santos," she murmured.

"It's the truth. If Alec had met you when he and I were roommates during our college days, *señora*, I believe I would have had no choice but to contest him for your affections."

"You were at college together?"

"University College, Oxford," he confirmed. "Alec was in the archaeology department, of course. I was studying social environmentalism."

K.J. tried to recall if Alec had told her he'd attended Oxford, then realized that even if he had, she undoubtedly wouldn't have heard him. Her mind, at the time, had not exactly been on his academic credentials.

"What, exactly, is social environmentalism?" she asked Rafael in a way that reminded Alec of how fascinated she'd seemed that night in the hotel bar, while he'd been discussing his work. And this expedition.

"It's a bit complex, utilizing all the social sciences, but what it mostly boils down to is a study of man's relationship to his environment. And how to make room for a burgeoning population on an increasingly fragile planet."

"I'm intrigued." She took a longer, more judicial look at the man who appeared so comfortable in the loosely woven shirt and trousers. "I don't believe I've ever met an Oxford man."

"You've met me," Alec reminded her. "Besides," he said through clenched teeth, hating the way Kate was gazing up at Rafael admiringly, "it's not that big a deal. Lots of people go to Oxford."

"I certainly don't meet that many," she countered with false sweetness, thoroughly enjoying the way her innocent interest in his friend seemed to be irritating Alec so.

She turned her attention back to Rafael. "And since I've always donated to environmental causes, I find what you're trying to do very admirable."

"It's not as if I have much choice if I want to save both the rain forest and my people."

"Your people?" She glanced around the cantina, which now had many more customers than when she'd first arrived. Obviously, K.J. realized, she was proving a curiosity in Santa Clara. "I assumed from your name that you were of Spanish descent."

"On my father's side. My mother was Indian. And, before her death, the royal princess."

"Really?" Once again her rapt expression had Alec grinding his teeth. "Would that make you a prince?"

"Technically, I suppose it would," Rafael said modestly. "Our people are a matriarchal society, but since I don't have any sisters, the tribe decided to send me out into civilization to learn the new ways to keep them from extinction."

"I'm very impressed. I've never met a king before, either."

"Prince," he corrected easily. "And believe me, Señora Mackenzie, it's not all that impressive."

"And it's a small tribe," Alec grunted, hating the way Kate was smiling up at Rafael like some beauty queen trying to win a judge's vote at a pageant.

Rafael's lips twitched ever so slightly at his friend's irritated tone. "True. And we're not nearly as wealthy as the European or Middle Eastern ones that normally come to mind when you think of royalty. But so far, despite so many of our people marrying into the Spanish community, we've managed to survive and keep much of our culture intact. Which some consider a miracle in itself."

If Rafael was at all uncomfortable at the tension arcing between Alec and K.J., he didn't show it. He glanced over at his college friend. "I assume you've told Kate about the festival?"

"I was just starting to," Alec all but growled as the green-eyed monster's claws dug a little deeper into his gut at the sound of his own private name for his wife on his best friend's lips.

Deciding to pay him back just a little bit more for the sexy barmaid, K.J. continued to ignore Alec as she smiled up at the mahogany man with the dark, sexy eyes. "From Alec's description, the festival sounds absolutely fascinating."

"I suppose fascinating is in the eye of the beholder," Rafael said mildly, this time not quite repressing a grin that was obviously at Alec's expense.

Alec was seething. Before Rafael's arrival at their table, Kate had been openly disinterested in the festival. More than that, she'd seemed dead set against attending. Now she was looking as if she'd just been given an invitation to a Mardi Gras ball in Rio.

"How long does it last?" K.J. asked.

"Three days. It starts at sundown tomorrow night. By then all the tourists will have flown in."

"Flown in? On a plane?" Her spine, which had begun to sag earlier, turned as stiff as a Highlander's spear. "There's a way to fly into here?"

"Of course," Rafael assured her. "Although we're not exactly a hub of civilization, the village does need supplies. And the ability to airlift someone out if they're hurt or sick. The airstrip isn't big enough for commercial jets, but it can handle the charter planes that bring in food, clothing and medicine. And, these days, tourists interested in observing one of the world's last living Stone Age tribes."

"A plane," K.J. repeated numbly.

Awaiting the fireworks, Alec shrugged his shoulders and took another long swallow of beer.

"The airstrip's proven quite handy," Rafael divulged. "It's made our tourist trade possible."

"An airstrip," she repeated flatly. "For the tourists."

"Not many *turistas* are willing to risk traveling on the river," Rafael said

"Gee. I wonder why not?" she asked dryly, thinking back over her own dangerous journey. "To tell the truth, I'm amazed a place this far from civilization gets many tourists."

"Actually, we've become a popular destination among those wealthy Americans, Europeans and Japanese who've grown tired of the usual jet-setting haunts," Rafael responded. "Even Kenya is in danger of being overdone. This is about the last unspoiled destination on earth."

"You certainly won't get any argument from me there," K.J. agreed. "So is tourism how the tribe survives these days?" She thought that a bit sad, even if perhaps it did help keep the culture alive.

"In the short term. Although it hasn't been easy, I've convinced the elders to give up the old slash-and-burn agriculture that's been destroying the forest. In the long term, we're negotiating several contracts with various American and French pharmaceutical companies who are turning to our native plants in hopes of finding cures for cancer and other illnesses. Meanwhile, before that money starts coming in, we decided to cater to the booming adventure tourism crowd."

"Which brings us back to that airstrip," she murmured. She put her elbows on the table and lowered her head to her hands. "Where planes land. Loaded with rich tourists."

Alec and Rafael exchanged a look, Rafael seeming less than pleased with the deception that had caused her such obvious misery. For his part, Alec sat back and wondered when he'd become the kind of bastard who could actually enjoy watching a beautiful woman's distress.

When she finally lifted her gaze to his, her eyes shot furious sparks that reminded him that his Campbell wife was not as fragile as her reed-slender appearance might suggest.

"Why didn't your agent mention that I could just fly into the village?"

"I have no idea," Alec lied, lifting his shoulders in a careless shrug. "Actually, I'm not certain I ever mentioned the airstrip to her, since she wasn't planning on making the trip herself."

K.J. gave him another long look. "Why do I not entirely buy that story?"

"Beats me." He gave her his most sincere smile in return. "I suppose it has something to do with your exhaustion. It's always harder to think logically when you're still suffering from jet lag."

"I never get jet lag. And I'm always logical."

Alec couldn't help smiling. "Not always," he corrected. Then, before she could respond to that reminder of the rash, absolutely illogical night they'd shared, he stood up. "Come on, let's get you settled in before dinner."

She was looking at his outstretched hand as if she were Snow White and he was the wicked stepmother holding out the poisoned apple.

When she continued just to sit there, Alec plucked her hand from the tabletop, laced their fingers together and eased her to her feet.

Deciding that to shake loose of his possessive touch would only add to the gossip undoubtedly circulating around the village, she allowed her hand to stay in his. She said goodbye to Rafael, who assured her he was definitely looking forward to seeing her later, then left the building with Alec.

As steamy as it had been inside, the bright sun an

suffocating heat hit like a fist as they came out of the dark cantina. Although he'd long since grown accustomed to the breath-stealing humidity, Alec felt Kate sway beside him.

"Want to go back inside?" He put a supportive arm around her waist.

"No." Once more he had to give her credit for being a lot tougher than she looked. He felt her stiffen beneath his hand, watched her luscious mouth pull into a grim, determined line. "I'll be fine. Really."

He gave her another long look, then decided that if she did decide to faint on him, he'd have no trouble picking her up. She was, if anything, even more slender than she'd been when he'd carried her over the threshold of his hotel room.

"Your call." He began walking, shortening his usually long-legged stride for her benefit.

As she realized he was leading her even farther away from the river, K.J. looked back toward the lush green bank. "My bags—"

"Don't worry. They've been taken care of."

"They've been taken to the lodge?"

"I thought we'd settled on the fact that the lodge is all booked up."

"Well, I know that's what the boatman—"

"Raul," Alec corrected quietly, but firmly.

"That's what Raul said." She stressed the man's name and received a satisfied nod in response. "But I thought that with your obvious influence, and being friends with the prince and all, surely you'd be able to do something."

"Like wave my magic wand and make a luxury suite appear?" He shook his head. "Sorry, sweetheart, but there isn't a bed to be had. But you wouldn't like the lodge, anyway, because it's set up dormitory style. No privacy."

"Oh." She thought that over for a moment. Then, although she'd shoved the dark glasses back onto her face, Alec imagined he could see the suspicion darkening her eyes again as she stopped in her tracks and looked up at him. "So where will I be spending the night?"

"The obvious place, of course," he answered. His wicked grin dared K.J. to offer a single word of complaint. "With your beloved husband."

She was too exhausted to argue that point at the moment. As he led her through the jungle, K.J. felt a lot like Deborah Kerr being directed away from the perils of the African jungle by Stewart Granger, in *King Solomon's Mines.* Coincidentally, she'd seen the movie on late-night cable just a few days before she'd stupidly agreed to track Alec down and bring him to New York for the bachelor auction.

Much of the overhead vegetation had been cleared from the village center. But here, beyond the gathering of huts, the multiple level of trees overhead created a lush green canopy that resembled leafy Gothic buttresses.

"How far are we going?" she asked, refusing to show weakness by complaining, but desperately hoping that Alec's hut was somewhere close by. When her foot slipped on a moss-covered branch, she reached out to steady herself and then cried out when she pricked her hand.

Alec turned around at her faint cry, realizing what she'd done. "Damn," he muttered. "I should have thought to warn you not to touch anything. Especially one of these give-and-take trees."

K.J. watched as he took a deadly looking knife from

a leather sheath on his belt and, being careful to avoid the needlelike spines, sliced off a piece of outer bark from a nearby tree.

"This will fix you right up." He took hold of her burning hand with a surprisingly tender touch and dabbed a bit of the gauzelike inner bark on her palm and the base of her fingers. When he lifted her hand up to his mouth and blew lightly on that sensitive skin, K.J. felt a flare of heat that had nothing to do with her injury. "Feel better?"

Actually, it did. "That's amazing."

"The jungle can be a vicious place." Alec resisted, just barely, the urge to press his lips against that pale smooth flesh he was holding in his. "But it's also generous with its cures. To those who know how to use them."

"And you do?" She decided that since he didn't seem in any hurry to release her hand, she may as well stop tugging on it. There was, after all, no point in antagonizing the man who seemed to possess the only spare bed in the village.

When another soft breath soothed the injury like a gentle summer zephyr across her flesh, K.J. wondered when she'd become such a liar. The only reason she wasn't fighting Alec holding her hand was because it felt so good. So right.

"I may not know the jungle vegetation as well as Rafael. But I do know enough to get by."

Her hands were just as he'd remembered them. Slender, competent and unadorned with either colored lacquer or jewelry. He thought about the slender gold ring he still carried with him, remembered finding it atop the note on his pillow, and although that memory continued to irk, the vivid recollection of exactly how these soft hands had felt on his heated flesh steamrolled over the less appealing ones.

As they'd left the cantina, Alec had promised himself that he wouldn't touch her until she'd gotten some rest. That he wouldn't taste her until tomorrow, after the opening ceremony that was part actual tribal ritual, part choreography.

But as he touched his thumb to the silky skin at the inside of her wrist, watched the awareness rise in Kate's eyes and felt her pulse jump, Alec realized that some resolutions were doomed from the start.

## 7

K.J. STARED UP INTO the gray eyes that had turned stormy with masculine intent, and tried to tell herself that she would have backed away if she hadn't already learned it was dangerous not to look where you were going in this verdant land.

"Alec…" The protest hovered on the tip of her tongue, but she couldn't quite make herself say it.

"I like it when you say my name." He lifted her hand to his lips, kissing each fingertip in turn, causing her pulse to skip a beat, then begin hammering in her veins. "It reminds me of all the ways you said it that night." He turned her wrist and treated it to a kiss that caused the breath to clog in her lungs.

Assuring herself that the unrelenting humidity was the only thing affecting her breathing, K.J. tried again. "Alec—"

"Soft, like that," he said approvingly, forestalling her attempted protest. "In the beginning, it was like a promise." His free hand slipped into the waistband of her slacks, drawing her closer. "A prayer."

"Dammit, Alec—" She managed to get a bit more heat into her tone this time.

"That's exactly what you said when you complained that I was taking things too slow."

His long, wickedly clever fingers had inched between the sodden linen trousers and the hot, damp skin of her stomach. For his own pleasure—and ultimately hers, Alec assured himself—he inched his hand even lower.

"But I wanted our wedding night to be something we'd both remember for the rest of our lives." His caressing touch easily breached her panties, which were, like their owner, an intriguing contrast—practical cotton woven into a sexy, low-cut, barely there bikini.

He skimmed a hot path though those silken curls he remembered being the color of flame. She was trembling now, and rather than pushing him away, her free hand, the one that wasn't still captured in his, was clutching at his shoulder.

"If I'd known it was going to be nearly twelve long months before we'd have an encore, I would have just tied you to the bed with those sexy stockings you were wearing."

He could still remember the first time he'd taken her, wearing only those lace-topped stockings and her gleaming new wedding ring.

Realizing that she'd lost the opportunity to back away, and afraid that she was no longer capable of standing on her own, K.J. had no choice but to cling to Alec's broad shoulder.

"Stockings are more economical than panty hose," she managed to answer with a moan as she felt a roughened fingertip part the unbearably sensitive folds at the juncture of her thighs. "If one leg runs…"

Afraid she'd fall to the jungle floor, which undoubtedly wasn't quite the lush green carpet it appeared to be, K.J. pulled her other hand loose from his and held on to him for dear life. "You don't lose both…oh!" She gasped as that treacherous finger slipped inside her tight channel.

She could protest the reality of their marriage all she wanted, but her body damn well couldn't lie, Alec thought with satisfaction as it clutched at his finger like a greedy fist. She was hot and wet and ready.

"You were wet that night, too," he said, as a second finger slipped past those slick lower lips. "Just like now."

"It's the heat," she lied. "I'm wet all over."

"And hot."

He touched his mouth to the soft hollow in her throat, where her pulse fluttered as fast as a hummingbird's wings. When he skimmed the tip of his tongue along her throat, gathering up the beaded moisture, a soft sound that was part sigh, part whimper escaped her lips. Lips he still hadn't tasted, Alec reminded himself.

"You can't deny that some of this heat is for me, Kate."

She wished he'd stop calling her that name that brought back so many sensual memories. Wished he'd stop touching her. Hoped he'd never stop.

"No." Her hips were moving instinctively against his intimate touch. "Of course I can't." Her breath had turned weak and shallow. "But...oh, God," she moaned, abandoning another intended protest as those wicked fingers delved deeper.

"We're good together, Kate." He gave up nibbling at her earlobe and seductively rubbed his mouth against hers. "We were that night." His lips plucked at hers. "And we're still good."

She murmured something that might have been a denial, were it not for the way one of her legs was now wrapping around his.

On the verge of exploding, and knowing that to press her back against a tree or drag her down onto the ground that was teeming with all sorts of unsavory insect life would be the height of irresponsibility,

Alec reluctantly decided that he had no choice but to end this now. Before it was too late.

"Better than good," he said, as he stroked the roughened pad of his thumb against the full, hard nub hidden in the folds of her sex. "Let go, sweetheart. Like you did that night."

K.J. couldn't help it. When she felt herself shattering, her breathless cry echoed through the jungle, scattering colorful birds from their branches overhead and earning chattering scolds from hidden monkeys. When she would have sunk to her knees, Alec pulled her tight against him, holding her up until the tremors finally ceased.

"I can't believe I did that," she gasped, when she could speak again.

"I can." He smiled down at her, with his lips and his eyes. "You were always as hot as a firecracker on the Fourth of July, Mrs. Mackenzie." He reluctantly retrieved his hand and zipped up the slacks he'd unfastened to give him more maneuvering room. "And since you claim to have been celibate these past months, you were definitely ready for liftoff."

"You have such a way with words," she muttered. She finally managed to back away. Not very far, but enough to break the hot and, heaven help her, all too enticing contact.

Beneath the worn jeans, he was obviously aroused. When she found herself wanting to drop to her knees and press her lips against that hard male bulge, K.J. fought even harder for control. This was, after all, a war of wills. A war she was determined to win.

"There are times I find it hard to believe you're actually a writer." She was proud when her voice had regained a bit of its usual strength.

"I explained that the first night. I'm a treasure hunter first. A writer second."

K.J. decided that this definitely wasn't the time to admit that somehow, while she'd been indulging in sexy daydreams about going upstairs to bed with this man, she'd missed that salient declaration.

"You're also the kind of man who'd be described in a historical romance as a rogue. Or a rake." Exactly the kind of man Helen Campbell would have barred the door against if he'd dared come calling for her grand-daughter.

"I suppose that's true enough." He snagged her waistband again and dragged her to him for another hard, hot kiss that left her reeling. "But I don't recall you complaining."

Because he was holding her so closely, K.J. had to tilt her head back to meet his challenging gaze. "Perhaps that's because you've never given me the oppor-tunity."

"Tell me that you really wanted me to stop and I'll apologize for what we just did and promise never to touch you again. Unless you ask."

"I'm not certain that's a good idea," she admitted reluctantly. "Since I seem to lose my head whenever you get within kissing distance." But not her heart, K.J. vowed. This time she was going to keep firm con-trol over that vital organ.

He chuckled and skimmed a finger along the seam of her now-frowning lips. "Believe me, sweetheart, I know the feeling. All too well." He lowered his head and kissed her again, the light touch of his mouth against hers no less stimulating than his earlier harsher kiss.

"So, to keep us both honest, if you want me to lay a

hand on your hot, lissome body, Mrs. Mackenzie, you'll have to beg."

"I've never begged for anything in my life."

For discretion's sake, Alec decided not to remind her of the way she'd done exactly that sometime just before dawn all those months ago.

"Well then…" He skimmed a finger down the slope of her nose. "You shouldn't have anything to worry about, should you?"

"No." She shouldn't, K.J. told herself, then wished she could actually believe her pitiful attempt at self-assurance. The regretful truth of the matter was that she didn't seem to have any restraint when it came to making love with this man. "Not at all."

That settled, at least for now, they continued on. They'd gone less than ten paces when Alec, who was leading the way, flashed her a quick grin over his shoulder.

"And by the way," he said, "when it comes to you, I don't seem to have a great deal of Highland pride in my veins. Which means that anytime you're in the mood, Mrs. Mackenzie, I'll be more than happy to beg."

Refusing to respond to that provocative declaration, K.J. wished Alec would stop calling her Mrs. Mackenzie. She also wished that if he was going to walk in front of her this way, he hadn't chosen to wear that particular pair of jeans.

When she found herself wanting to pounce on him, K.J. worried that if Alec stuck to his pledge not to touch her again, begging on her part might be inevitable.

His bamboo hut, with its tin roof, turned out to be much the same as the majority of the ones they'd passed. Except for one thing. Even as exhausted as she was, K.J. couldn't help smiling at the small round holes that had been dug in the cleared ground.

"Don't tell me," she murmured. "You've actually built a golf course."

"Not for the tourists. This is just for Rafael and me. We're not ready to have the Amazon Open," Alec allowed, returning her smile with a quick, dazzling grin of his own. "And the rough's a bit more challenging than Saint Andrews, but for what it is, it's not that bad."

"I know all about the Scots' passion for golf." Her father had certainly been addicted. "But don't you think this is carrying things a bit far?"

"Not really. Some putting practice at the end of the day helps clear my head. And if you want to discuss Scots' passions, believe me, Kate, golf definitely isn't at the top of my list."

He was looking at her that way again. That warm way that turned his storm gray eyes to pewter and made her unruly heart turn somersaults.

"You can't keep talking this way to me," she complained.

"Ah, but I'm no' the one who brought up a Scotsman's passions," he reminded her with an exaggerated burr as he opened the bamboo door.

"I happen to know you were born in Montana." At least she remembered that much.

"A Scot's a Scot wherever he's born," Alec argued. "You of all people should know that clan roots have a lot more to do with blood than geography. And believe me, darlin', any Scotsman worth his salt has a passion for wars, pipes, golf and bonny lassies running deep in his bones." He winked. "And not necessarily in that order."

The small house seemed to be a single room. It had

no square corners, which gave it the illusion of space. As did the high, tin ceiling. The room had been divided into various areas. The small, compact kitchen boasted a propane camp stove, a metal pan she assumed was used for washing dishes, a rustic table and two chairs that had been handcrafted from various woods.

He'd set up an office in another portion of the room. A laptop computer and camera equipment filled the shelves; maps and charts and graphs had been spread over a makeshift desk. Across from that, in what she took to be the bedroom, a large hemp hammock draped in gauzy mosquito netting hung from a ceiling beam. Someone, she assumed Raul, the boatman, had brought her bags to the hut and left them beside the hammock, next to a small bamboo chest.

Tacked to the wall was a group of strikingly familiar photographs. "I can't believe this."

"I told you that your father's photographs were particular favorites of mine."

"I thought you were lying."

"Why would I do that?"

She shrugged. "It's not such a bad pickup line."

"I've never resorted to pickup lines." He left unstated the fact that he certainly hadn't needed one that night. "Besides, I've never lied to you, Kate."

Her faint smile took the challenge out of the suspicious look she shot him. "How about the headhunters?"

"That may have been a bit of an embellishment," he allowed. "However, in my defense, you never really know what you're going to run across in the depths of this jungle. And for the record, I've never lied about my feelings for you."

"I believe you." She stopped in front of a particular

favorite, a dazzling display of bright colors, with elephants draped in gilt tapestries, women swathed in rainbow silk saris, men in sorbet turbans. "I remember when that was taken," she said with some surprise. "It was at the Pushkar Fair. I was six and we spent two months in India." She smiled at the memory. "It's an amazing place. I loved it."

"It's definitely one of the most complex, colorful, dense, spellbinding cultures on the planet," he agreed.

She glanced over at him. "You've been there?"

"Yeah. And had a great time. It's definitely not for control freaks, though. There's no shallow end of the pool there. You have to take the full body-and-soul plunge."

"Dad said you had to get into a 'go with the flow of the Ganges' mindset." Her smile widened at the memory, even as her eyes misted.

"Phantasmagoria." Alec's answering smile was warm and friendly, lacking its usual sexual edge. "The Indian suspension of intellectual control."

Finding it surprising that they'd have anything in common other than sex, K.J. moved on to the next photograph, where George Campbell had captured a fly fisherman casting a line in an icy winter stream. The starkness of the black, leafless trees and the heavy, wet falling snow actually made her shiver, despite the near-suffocating heat.

"Well, I can certainly see why you have that one up in here," she said.

"It reminds me of Montana."

"It was." It had also been six months before her parents had died, she recalled all too well.

"And, yeah, it works pretty well as mental air-conditioning, too. Your father had a genius at plunking viewers right down into the scene."

"He loved his work," she murmured.

"It shows." Alec paused a moment, as if choosing his words carefully. "It shows in your work, as well."

The fact that he'd actually bought two of her photographs both surprised and pleased K.J. "You didn't have these when we met," she murmured, looking at the shot she'd taken of a father and son flying a colorful dragon kite on a summer's day at the shore in Atlantic City. Beside it was the companion photograph, a close-up of the man's larger, darker hand atop his son's as they held on to the white cord.

"No. I went looking for something you'd done afterward. I bought more, but it's a little difficult to carry them all around with me at the same time. And I was concerned about damage from the humidity once we got into the rainy season."

The man was providing one surprise after another. "What other ones did you buy?"

"The old man's dog herding the sheep." She'd taken that on a rainy Saturday in Pennsylvania. "The dynamite head-on shot of the jockeys driving their horses to the finish line." Three wonderfully productive days at Saratoga.

"The little girl in the kimono pouring tea for an old woman." That shot had been taken at Japan House, the headquarters of the Japan Society, near the U.N. The woman—the child's grandmother—had apparently spent months instructing the little girl in the ancient tea ceremony.

"With an eye like yours, I'm amazed you're wasting your talent editing romance books."

"Very popular books," she reminded him stiffly. "And I don't consider it a waste of talent. A great many people—including me—receive pleasure from those novels. Instead of reading about ourselves men see us, romance novels reflect women's hopes, beliefs and values. I'm proud of my part in their creation.''

''Okay, I stand corrected. Perhaps it isn't a waste. And I have no doubt that you're a terrific editor, but special talent like your father's and yours is a two-edged sword, Kate. You have a responsibility to share your vision of the world.''

''I also have a responsibility to myself to eat. When my father was getting started, my mother's salary at the publishing house allowed him to buy the film and cameras he needed to do his best work. And paid for his travel, in the beginning.''

By the time her parents had died, a single George Campbell photograph could have easily supported a family of six for at least a year. Unfortunately, after her grandmother's death, K.J. had discovered that Helen Campbell had used nearly every cent of his estate to keep her white elephant of a mansion and equally large summer home running. K.J.'s entire inheritance had been roughly thirty thousand dollars, which, while a nice sum of money, still wasn't enough to allow her to take the financial risk of switching careers.

''I don't see the problem. Now that you have a filthy rich husband—which, in case I didn't mention it, I am—you can quit your day job.''

''I keep telling you, you're not really my husband.'' And even if their marriage was real, she wasn't certain her strong Campbell independent streak would allow her to let Alec financially support her career.

''Look at that next photograph. And try telling me that again,'' he suggested.

She sighed as she took in the photograph she remembered all too well. Which wasn't surprising, since ·he had a duplicate one hidden away in the drawer of her bedside table. It was a picture of her looking amazingly sexy and undeniably radiant in her scarlet-as-sin wedding dress.

A rebel to the core, Alec hadn't brought a suit to the writers' conference, but as she took in the sight of him in jeans and a white shirt, she found him every bit as dashing as she had that night. Which was, of course, a danger.

She also found it more than a little unsettling that he'd not only saved the photograph, as she had, but displayed it openly. The candid photograph had been taken by the minister's wife seconds before Kate and Alec had kissed for the first time as man and wife. Her face, framed by his large hands as she'd looked up at him, was nothing less than beatific. And although the shot lacked technical merit, it had still managed to capture, in stunning detail, exactly what she'd been feeling at that moment. It was love, pure and simple.

Not so simple, she corrected sadly.

Alec watched her trying not to study the photograph he'd been tormenting himself with for months. The fact that she'd failed was a good sign.

"You were the most beautiful woman I'd ever seen," he murmured huskily, coming up behind her.

"It was the dress," she said, briefly closing her eyes as she felt his warm breath teasing at her ear. "It was stunning."

"The dress was attractive." His hands curved over her shoulders, pulling her back against him as they both studied the photograph. "But it was the bride who was stunning."

The photograph had captured her at an uncensored moment, and only a blind man wouldn't have recognized the love shining in her eyes as she'd gazed up at him in that suspended instant before he'd kissed h

So what the hell had happened between that moment and the next morning?

It couldn't have been their lovemaking, Alec assured himself, as he had for months. There was no way she could have faked her avid, unrestrained response to him. To them together. By the time he'd taken her that last time in the shower, they'd both lost track of how many times she'd come.

"I don't want to quibble yet again," she murmured, slipping away from his light but possessive touch and turning away from that wall that held too many emotional memories. "But there seems to be only one hammock."

Alec bit down in frustration at the way she'd edged away, both physically and emotionally, and concentrated on the flush that colored her cheeks so prettily as she took in the hammock. Obviously, her imagination was as active as he remembered.

"Ah, the lass is observant as well as bonny," he said with that feigned Scots burr.

Her eyes flew to his dark, laughing ones. "Surely you don't expect me to sleep with you?"

"I don't know why not. You are, after all, my bride, Katherine Jeanne Campbell Mackenzie." He stressed, yet again, the name she'd so willingly taken that night.

"In name only."

"I may be accused of being a bit daft sometimes, darling. But I certainly couldn't forget consummating our marriage vows. And I know it wasn't a dream or a sexual fantasy, because believe me, even my imagination isn't that vivid." His grin was as wicked as she'd ever witnessed it.

"That was then. This is now."

"Don't worry." His smile lost its voltage, and shad- ws turned his formerly gleaming eyes to the gloomy color of thunderclouds hanging over a steely sea. "I'll bunk with Rafael for the night." He bit the words off, all warmth and affection gone from his tone. "And since I've never been into forcing myself on women, you don't have to concern yourself about your husband taking his conjugal rights while you're sleeping."

K.J. decided that the least she could do was give credit where credit was due. Particularly if she wanted to coax Alec into coming back to New York with her. This continual sparring couldn't be helpful to her cause.

"I doubt I'd ever be so exhausted I could sleep through that," she murmured.

His lips tilted and renewed humor chased away the shadows from his eyes. "Is that a compliment I hear coming from those eminently kissable lips?"

Because she knew she'd never get away with a lie, K.J. opted to tell the truth. Or at least a bit of it. "You were a wonderful lover, Alec. But there's more to life—and marriage—than sex."

"That's true enough, I suppose," he said vaguely. "But you can't deny that it's not a bad foundation to build on."

Because it had been too long since he'd tasted her, and to prove to the both of them that she wasn't any more immune to the electricity arcing between them than he was, Alec ducked his head and once again covered her frowning mouth with his.

# 8

HER FIRST MURMUR sounded vaguely like a protest, but unwilling to surrender control, Alec refused to retreat. As he lingered over the kiss, gentled it, he was pleased by the way Kate sank so quickly, so willingly into it.

Without taking her mouth from his, she went up on her toes, dragged her hands through his hair and parted her lips, inviting him to take the kiss deeper. Which he did. His tongue slipped inside the sweet warmth, stroking, exploring, thrilling.

Heaven help her, he was every bit as solid as she remembered, and although he was a good head taller, they fit together as perfectly as they had in all the sexy dreams she'd been suffering through these past months.

Alec's taste was as dark and as potent as Scotch whisky, possessing the power to make her head spin and her knees weaken. Desire flared from smoldering embers she'd tried to convince herself had cooled.

*This is ridiculously foolish,* her internal nag warned. *You'll never succeed in getting the man to agree to that divorce if you turn to putty every time he kisses you.*

For a fleeting, reckless moment, K.J. wondered if it would be so wrong, so foolish, not to insist on a divorce, as she'd intended. How could she turn her back on such pleasure? she asked herself. How could she walk away from this?

Then he lifted his head and broke the blissful contact of their mouths, causing her soaring mind to come crashing back to earth—and reality—with a bang.

"You broke your promise." The afternoon rain had begun; K.J. could hear it pounding like machine-gun fire on the tin roof.

"No, I didn't," Alec countered. "I promised not to touch you. And I didn't. My hands were behind my back the entire time."

Not that he'd had much choice, since it had either been that or give in to impulse and rip those wrinkled clothes from her soft yielding flesh, Alec admitted to himself wryly.

They stood there, toe-to-toe, Alec looking down at her, K.J. looking back up at him. For a suspended moment the world around them seemed to fade away as old memories warred with current circumstances.

Alec was the first to break the silence. "Kate?"

Only a deaf woman would not have heard the desire in his gruff voice. A desire, heaven help her, that was also burning hot and deep inside her.

"What now?" she snapped, when she wanted to weep.

"I think, in the interest of fair play, you'd better consider this a warning."

"What kind of warning?"

As she stared up into his fierce eyes, flashes of sensual images—memories of all they'd done together—assaulted her like a shower of stones.

"If you don't say something right now to stop me, I'm going to go back on my word not to touch you."

*Oh yes*, she wanted to cry out. *Touch me. Taste me. Take me. Now.* Needs tugged at her, seductive and unrelenting.

"I don't want you to touch me." Her voice w weak and ragged.

It was a lie. And they both knew it.

But circumstances, heat and exhaustion stepped in to replace the willpower that seemed to have deserted her. K.J. had no sooner gotten the words out of her mouth when she went strangely light-headed. The room began to spin around in circles, and for the first time in her life, she felt as if she was going to faint. She began to sway, as little white dots danced like fireflies around her head.

"Hell, you'd better lie down before you fall down." Although she was not a petite woman, he scooped her into his arms as if she weighed no more than a handful of feathers.

"That's ridiculous. I've never fainted in my life," she argued. Her cheek was resting on the hard wall of his chest. His heartbeat was strong and, she feared, a great deal steadier than hers.

"There's always a first time for everything." He pulled back the mosquito netting and carefully lowered her to the hammock. "And having that beer when you were bound to be dehydrated undoubtedly didn't help matters any. I shouldn't have encouraged you to drink it."

She opened her eyes and looked straight into his. "That wasn't your decision to make."

He shook his head, his faint smile suggesting that he found it amusing she could summon up the energy to argue even now when she was on the verge of passing out.

"Shut up." He skimmed his fingers up the side of her face, then brushed some damp hair off her forehead. "And although I realize you're a strong-minded, independent female who doesn't need to be what to do, I'm going to risk your Campbell wrath by suggesting that you'll feel a lot better after a nap."

"I suppose that sounds like a sensible idea," she admitted. And anyone who knew her would tell you that K.J. Campbell was nothing if not sensible. Well, at least most of the time. Rushing off to the jungle in hopes of a promotion probably wasn't the most prudent thing she'd ever done in her life. And certainly eloping with Alec had not even come close to sensible.

"Would you like something to eat before I leave you alone?"

From what she'd sampled thus far, jungle cuisine wasn't exactly five-star. Deciding that she wasn't on the verge of starving anytime soon, K.J. allowed her achingly heavy eyelids to drift shut.

"No, thank you," she said politely. The hemp rope hammock was surprisingly comfortable. She curled up in it and snuggled down for the duration. "I'll be…fine." Her words slowed along with her breathing. "I just…need…to rest my eyes…for a little bit. Then we really do need to talk about… You know."

"Making love?"

"No. And shame on you for taking advantage…of my temporarily weakened condition." The faint curve of her lips took the heat out of the accusation.

"Sorry."

He didn't sound at all like he meant it, but too tired to argue, K.J. decided to give him the benefit of the doubt. "You're forgiven."

She was drifting away, feeling as if she were sinking into soft fluffy clouds. At first she thought she might have imagined the butterfly light touch on her templ then realized it was his lips brushing against her sl It was then K.J. realized that, although she'd kr he was strong and forceful and dangerously charismatic, she hadn't realized he could also be heartbreakingly gentle.

And it was that surprising tenderness she most needed to guard against.

With that warning floating through the filmy ether of her mind, K.J. temporarily surrendered the battle and allowed sleep to claim her.

Alec sat across the room watching his wife while she slept. The same way he had the morning after their marriage. Except that day he hadn't been forced to study her from a distance, because she'd been snuggled in his arms like a soft warm kitten.

The diaphanous netting did not prevent him from seeing the way her breasts rose and fell beneath the thin cotton T-shirt. Alec remembered all too well how they'd fit so perfectly into his hands, how the undersides were as smooth and pale as the snowy white roses he'd actually thought to pick up in the hotel's Canterbury Florist Shop for her bouquet.

He had no trouble recalling the scent of her silky skin, or its taste. The memory of how her rosy nipple had turned hard as a stone between his gently tugging teeth caused a sexual ache that went all the way to the bone.

He knew that no matter how human beings might wish otherwise, time marched inexorably along, ticking off minutes, hours, days, months, years, eons. But if the gods had suddenly decided to bestow superpowers on him that morning, looking back, Alec decided that if he'd known how things would have ended up, he would have unhesitatingly chosen the ability to freeze time in its tracks.

Before that damn argument. Before they'd both said ngs they didn't mean. Before he'd acted like a jerk.

And especially before she'd run off, back to her safe, predictable routine at that New York publishing house.

That had admittedly surprised him, especially after she'd shown such excitement about his work. He couldn't understand how a human being could stand to be locked within four walls all day long. He'd certainly go stark raving mad before six months had passed.

Although others might find his passion for treasure hunting more than a little quixotic, Alec had always considered his second career eminently reasonable. After all, he never took off to the back of beyond on a whim. On the contrary, he'd always prided himself on planning out an expedition down to the most minute detail. Admittedly, unforseen events inevitably blew a lot of those plans out of the water, but he'd never considered himself a man given to impulsive behavior.

Until that evening he'd entered the French rococo gilded banquet room of the Las Vegas Whitfield Palace Hotel, dreading a long-drawn-out meal of stuffed leather chicken and boring speeches, and seen an angel with a Highland lass's face staring back at him.

For the first time in his life, he hadn't given any thought to what he was doing. Hadn't been at all concerned with the consequences of his rash act. The only thing he'd known was that he wanted the woman with the fiery hair and eyes as blue as a loch beneath a rare summer sun.

And not just for one night. As he'd crossed the marble floor between them, he'd realized with not a little amazement that he wanted to claim her—as one of the Mackenzie lairds might have kidnapped a winsome woman from some enemy's clan—and keep her all his own.

The long intimate conversation later in the cocktail lounge had only confirmed that feeling. So, even as unplanned as it was, marriage had seemed an eminently logical solution.

She'd certainly not uttered a single word of protest, Alec thought now. Not when he'd shepherded her from Lancelot's Lounge, or later, when they'd entered that chapel and discovered that they were going to be married by Merlin the Magician and serenaded by three costumed guys playing mandolins and wearing purple tights.

But Kate hadn't seemed to care in the least. In fact, later, back in his suite, they'd laughed until their sides had ached.

And although the Scots were a pragmatic race, as he'd taken her into his arms and kissed her with a depth of emotion he'd never felt toward any other woman, Alec had known they were fated to be together.

Looking at her now, emotions welled up inside him, stunning him with their intensity. Shaken as he was by the force of the atypical feelings battering away at him, which for a multitude of reasons he wasn't going to take time to sort out right now, Alec realized that he'd told Kate the absolute truth when he'd sworn to hold her to their marriage vows.

She was his wife, dammit. And now that he had her back where she belonged, he wasn't going to let go of her.

The only problem, Alec reminded himself, was that the lady had already been spooked before. He didn't want her racing off, because this time he'd have to go after her. Like it or not, if he couldn't find the barge before another mudslide buried it even deeper, he'd have to give up this expedition. Which he was prepared to do, if it came down to a choice between Kate and the treasure.

But Alec was realizing that, although he would have once argued otherwise, he was a greedy man. He wanted Kate and he wanted the treasure. And he was determined to have both.

The thing to do, he decided, was to avoid giving her any more insights into his thoughts.

Although he had no intention of complying with her request for a divorce, it stood to reason that the longer he let her believe he might eventually give in, the longer she'd have to stay here in the jungle. Which would give him time to change her mind. To prove to her that they belonged together.

It wasn't much of a plan, Alec allowed as he employed all of his willpower not to join his sleeping bride in that hammock that had been too lonely for too long. But it would have to do until he could come up with a better one.

K.J. HAD NO IDEA how long she'd slept. For a moment, when she first awakened, she forgot where she was, but then she forced her still-heavy eyelids open and found herself staring straight into Alec's shuttered gray eyes.

"You're still here?"

"Seem to be."

She combed her fingers through the thick wavy tangles, almost grateful when some leaves and moss fell out that she didn't have a mirror handy. "How long did I sleep?"

"About three hours."

"Three hours?" She was stunned. She'd always possessed the ability to take quick, refreshing catnaps during the day, wherever she was, but to think of be ing dead to the world for so long… A thought occurred to her.

"Were you watching me all that time?"

"Yes."

"Why?"

"I like looking at you, Kate. And, after all this time apart, any man would enjoy the appealing sight of his wife back in his bed."

"We really need to talk about that, Alec." Since her head was clearer, K.J. decided to just come straight to the point.

"We can talk about all that later," he said, brushing her carefully spoken words away with a flick of a dark hand, as if they were a pesky fly he didn't want to bother with. "I imagine, after your travels, you might like to take a shower before dinner."

"A shower?" It sounded like heaven. Even better than the nap. Although the idea of taking off her clothes anywhere around Alec was a little disconcerting.

"While it's not exactly the Las Vegas Whitfield Palace, your Chez Mackenzie jungle accommodations also come with a shower. Of sorts."

"A shower," she repeated. She'd begun to fear that that little plumbing feature she so took for granted back home didn't exist anywhere in the jungle. Not even his mention of the hotel where they'd spent their one-night honeymoon could dampen her enthusiasm. "I think I love you." The words slipped out before she could censor them or call them back.

"Love's always a plus," he said, "in a marriage." From his mild tone he seemed suspiciously oblivious to the instant look of regret on her face about her verbal slip. "And in the interest of full disclosure, I suppose this is where I admit that the shower room isn't exactly attached to the hut. Actually, it's next to the privy."

"The privy." K.J. swore that when she returned to the States, she'd never take a flush toilet for granted again.

"You can't miss it. It's a six-holer, which makes it bigger than the average campsite one you're probably used to."

K.J. decided this was not the time to tell him that she hadn't been camping since she was nine years old and had gone to live with her grandmother, who considered sleeping on the ground and cooking meals over a campfire uncivilized. And Helen Campbell was nothing if not civilized.

Well, there had been that horse camp in Newport she'd talked her grandmother into letting her attend the summer she turned twelve. But K.J. doubted that really counted as camping, since all the little equestrians had slept on cotton sheets as smooth as silk, and meals had been catered from a local resort.

His description belatedly sunk in. "A six-holer? Are you saying the privy's communal?"

"Sure."

She closed her eyes, praying for patience. "Please tell me it's not unisex."

"Actually, it is." He waited a beat, feeling a faint prick of guilt at her weak moan of distress. "Usually. But because everyone understands that being from the outside world, you're not quite used to such familiarity, they're willing to make that one ladies only."

Well, at least that was something, K.J. thought, reminding herself that it was still better than hiding behind a tree the way she'd had to do during the trip downriver.

"And the ladies have also agreed, for now, to keep it to one visitor at a time."

"Thank you." This time it was K.J. who instigated a brief kiss. It was little more than a brush of lips against lips, but still packed one helluva punch. "For the privacy. And the shower. After the past few days, I think I'd surrender my soul for a chance to wash my hair."

"I doubt if you'll have to go that far," he said easily, as he linked their fingers together and led her back out the door. "I'm willing to settle for your heart."

Her heart. As she felt it turn flips at the light touch of his hand on her shoulder, K.J. feared that she'd never really gotten it back when she'd left Las Vegas last year.

After demonstrating how to operate the shower, which, he explained, was attached to an oil drum filled with rainwater, Alec left K.J. alone with her guilt.

"It's not as if I haven't been straight with him," she muttered as she lathered herbal shampoo through her hair for the first time in days. "I told him that I wanted a divorce."

*Sure, you tell him that,* her internal scold agreed scornfully. *Then you turn to jelly whenever he so much as looks at you. And in case you didn't think I saw it, it was you who initiated that last kiss.*

"It was a spontaneous gesture of gratitude."

*You didn't kiss the plumber who fixed your stopped-up sink last month,* the nagging little voice reminded her. *Or the waiter at that Greek restaurant who flirted with you, then gave you the complimentary order of rice pudding to take home. Or the bus driver who waited for you to run to the stop—*

"The bus driver was a woman."

*That's a moot point. And don't try to sidetrack me, be-*

*cause it won't work, Katherine Jeanne Campbell. Don't forget, I've known you since before you were born. In fact, I was already well established in your genetic makeup while you were still splitting cells.*

"Then how come you kept quiet for so many years?"

*In the beginning, your foolish parents' voices spoke louder than mine, so you couldn't hear me. Later, you had your grandmother to keep you in line. Now, like it or not, I'm all you've got. And I can tell when you're lying to yourself.*

"I'm not lying." Not really, she assured herself.

*You're not being entirely honest, either. You want the man, the same way you wanted him that night I warned you about what happens to women who let themselves get picked up by men in bars.*

"It wasn't a bar. Lancelot's Lounge was a very respectable cocktail lounge in one of the finest hotels in the country," she argued.

*Whatever. The point is that wine he plied you with obviously made you weak. And vulnerable.*

"No." K.J. stood beneath the stream of water and rinsed the fragrant suds from her hair. "Alec was the one who made me weak. The wine didn't have anything to do with it. Besides, I only had a single glass of merlot." She hadn't needed alcohol to make her feel as high as a kite.

*And now, after only a few hours together, he's having the same effect on you.*

"Unfortunately, that seems to be true." K.J. tilted her head back, enjoying the sensual feel of the water sluicing over her body. When she imagined it was Alec's hands creating such physical bliss, she was shaken by the surge of what could only be described as primal lust.

# PLAY BANGO!

## AND GET THREE FREE GIFTS!

**It looks like BINGO, it plays like BINGO but it's FREE!**

## HOW TO PLAY:

1. With a coin, scratch the Caller Card to reveal your 5 lucky numbers and see that they match your Bango Card. Then check the claim chart to discover what we have for you — FREE BOOKS and a FREE GIFT. All yours, all free!

2. Send back the Bango card and you'll receive 2 brand-new Harlequin Temptation® novels. These books have a cover price of $3.75 each in the U.S. and $4.25 each in Canada, but they are yours to keep absolutely free.

3. There's no catch. You're under no obligation to buy anything. We charge nothing — ZERO — for your first shipment. And you don't have to make any minimum number of purchases — not even one!

4. The fact is, thousands of readers enjoy receiving books by mail from the Harlequin Reader Service® months before they are available in stores. They like the convenience of home delivery and they love our discount prices!

5. We hope that after receiving your free books you'll want to remain a subscriber. But the choice is yours — to continue or cancel, any time at all! So why not take us up on our invitation, with no risk of any kind. You'll be glad you did!

## YOURS FREE!

**This exciting mystery gift is yours free when you play BANGO!**

# It's fun, and we're giving away
# FREE GIFTS
## to all players!

**PLAY BANGO!**

SCRATCH HERE! →

**CALLER CARD**

**YES!** Please send me all the free books and the gift for which I qualify! I understand that I am under no obligation to purchase any books as explained on the back of this card.

YOUR CARD ↘

**BANGO**

| 38 | 9 | 44 | 10 | 38 |
|----|----|------|----|----|
| 92 | 7 | 5 | 27 | 14 |
| 2 | 51 | FREE | 91 | 67 |
| 75 | 3 | 12 | 20 | 13 |
| 6 | 15 | 26 | 50 | 31 |

## CLAIM CHART!

| Match 5 numbers | 2 FREE BOOKS & A MYSTERY GIFT |
|-----------------|-------------------------------|
| Match 4 numbers | 2 FREE BOOKS |
| Match 3 numbers | 1 FREE BOOK |

(H-T-02/99)
**142 HDL CNG2**

**342 HDL CNHF**

Name: _____
(PLEASE PRINT)

Address: _____ Apt.#: _____

City: _____ State/Prov.: _____ Postal Zip/Code: _____

"But would that be so bad?" she asked rhetorically. "Having a fling with him? After all, we are married. Technically."

*Women don't have flings with their husbands.* The voice was as stern as her grandmother's had been that first summer, when K.J. had tried to gain favor by weeding the estate's garden and had pulled out the newly sprouted perennials instead.

"If that's true, then it may explain the divorce rate."

Although she could have let the needles of water pound out the tension in her body for the rest of the night, K.J. turned off the faucet, concerned about using up all his water, then took down a towel from a nearby bamboo shelf and wrapped it around her.

"We're both adults." She continued the rhetorical argument, wondering who she was trying harder to convince—that nagging little scold in the back of her mind, or herself. "And, as Alec keeps insisting on pointing out, we are married—"

*Technically,* the voice piped up, throwing her own word back at her. *You haven't lived a single full day as husband and wife.*

"True." And K.J. knew that years from now, when she was an old woman looking back at her life, that would be one of her biggest regrets.

But although she might not have a working model of marriage to emulate, she did know that it took two people to make a home. And by taking off the day after their wedding, he'd shown himself to have scant interest in either a home or family.

Not wanting to dilute her argument with emotion, K.J. refused to admit exactly how much like her father Alec was. Although in her parents' case, her mother hadn't hesitated to leave the security of her job and follow her husband around the world.

*And look how that turned out.*

"I really hate it when you read my mind," K.J grumbled.

*I am your mind,* the voice countered.

Belatedly realizing that she hadn't brought any fresh clothing out to the shower hut with her, K.J. dressed again in the rumpled T-shirt and slacks, forgoing her sweaty underwear. For the first time since her fourteenth birthday, she was grateful that Mother Nature hadn't been all that generous when gifting her with breasts. Hopefully, Alec wouldn't notice that she wasn't wearing a bra.

"Perhaps we could give it a second try," she considered, returning to the subject of her and Alec's marriage. After all, they'd both lost their tempers that morning. And they were both hardheaded, strongwilled individuals, each unwilling to concede defeat. Perhaps, if they could at least try to put that horrid argument behind them…

*Are you actually saying that you're willing to give up all the creature comforts of the city and move into a little grass shack with that man?*

"No. I'm saying that I'm willing to spend a few days—and nights—with him." Very sexy nights.

*Surely you're not considering stooping to using sex to seduce him into giving in to you?*

"Of course I'm not," K.J. said. "That would be too much like prostitution. Even though we have a marriage license." Signed by a man dressed in royal blue velvet robes with silver lamé stars sewn all over it. "Besides, I wouldn't know how to seduce a man."

Indeed, that night, although she hadn't been a virgin, K.J. had worried that she wouldn't be able to sexually satisfy Alec. But if his body hadn't lied—and she certainly didn't see how it could have faked such response—she'd amazed herself by living up to the sensual challenge.

"I won't push things," she decided. "I'll just let nature take its course. Then, after we get rid of all this sexual tension, Alec will undoubtedly be more amenable to the idea of returning to New York for the auction."

*Although I hate to give him credit for anything, I honestly can't see Alec Mackenzie displaying himself in front of a roomful of man-hungry women.*

"It won't last long. And it's for a good cause."

*Well, good luck,* the scold said sarcastically. *Because believe me, Katherine Jeanne, you're definitely going to need all you can get.*

Although she feared the annoying little nag was right, as she left the shower hut, K.J. wished that one of them felt just a bit more optimistic.

# 9

THE FIRST THING K.J. noticed when she returned to the hut was that Alec was still there, sitting at the table, his attention on the screen of the laptop computer, which he'd hooked up to a car battery. The second thing was the enticing aroma that filled the compact room.

"Is that dinner I smell?"

"Yeah." He glanced up. "I figured you might not be up to eating with everyone in the communal dining lodge after your long trip, so I rounded up a light meal for you."

"It doesn't include termites, does it?"

"Damn." He slapped his forehead. "Did you want a side of termites?" He pushed back from the table and stood up. "If you'll just wait a minute, I'll go out to that mound at the edge of the village and—"

"No!" She caught his arm as he was about to pass her on the way to the door. "I don't really want any termites."

"Okay. How about some beetles? They're a little crunchy, but there's nothing tastier than a deep-fried borer beetle dipped in hot sauce."

He was kidding, K.J. assured herself. Surely he didn't actually expect her to eat insects? She couldn't help wondering if her mother had ever been forced to such extremes on similar excursions.

"They sound delicious," she said with a false smile.

Just in case this was a test, K.J. was determined to pass. "However, I'm really not all that hungry, and fried food is so filling. And fattening."

"Whatever you say. Though a few more pounds wouldn't hurt."

Even as she reminded herself that continuing to spar with a man was not exactly the way to win him over, K.J. splayed her hands on her hips. "Are you calling me skinny?"

He cocked his head and studied her, his piercing, cool eyes treating her to an unnervingly long, slow appraisal that began at her freshly washed hair, which she could feel curling into unruly springs, down to her feet, which were clad in a very unsexy pair of hiking boots that the man in the outfitters store had assured her she'd need to protect her feet from all sorts of unsavory-sounding things animal, vegetable and mineral.

Seconds ticked by as those cool gray eyes returned to her face. "Well, you may have gotten a little scrawny—"

"Scrawny?"

"But you definitely still have curves in all the right places," he said encouragingly.

"I'm so pleased you approve." K.J. knew that compared to Sonia, the voluptuous, sloe-eyed barmaid, she'd definitely come out on the short end of the stick. Even worse. There was no comparison.

"Still, a little more meat on your bones wouldn't hurt all that much." When his eyes drifted back to her breasts, K.J. had to fight the ridiculous impulse to arch her spine to give them a bit more thrust. "You've lost weight, Kate."

"I have not." What on earth was the matter with

her? How was she going to get him to agree to a divorce if she kept arguing with everything he said?

Alec ignored her crisp denial. He just kept looking straight at her unfettered breasts and, although there wasn't a sign of lust in the judicious study, that didn't stop her traitorous nipples from hardening.

Refusing to cover herself with her arms, she stood there, still as a fence post, letting him look all he wanted, appearing as cool as the sensible adult woman she was, all the while wondering desperately if he could see the way those tingling nipples were pushing against the cotton of her T-shirt.

Alec could. And as his fingers itched to touch, he felt a similar tightening in his loins. "I'd say ten, maybe even fifteen pounds," he guessed, using those itchy fingers to rub his stubbled chin to prevent them from doing something rash.

"Obviously your memory's faulty." She lifted her chin in a way that would have put them eye-to-eye if his hadn't been moving with aching slowness back down her body.

"Nah. I have an eidetic memory. I remember everything." He paused a significant heartbeat. "Absolutely everything."

That wicked warrior's gaze lingered significantly at the juncture of her thighs in a way that had her vividly recalling well how much time he'd spent down there. Apparently, K.J. thought, biting back a moan with fierce determination, he wasn't the only one with a photographic memory. The way Alec was looking at her, along with the raw huskiness in his voice, caused moisture to pool thickly in that secret place.

She struggled gamely for control. "I may have lost a couple pounds." More like twelve, but she certainly wasn't going to give him the satisfaction of knowing how close he'd come. "But women's weights fluctuate all the time—we all have closets filled with different clothes for our fat and skinny days—so it doesn't really mean anything."

No way was she going to admit that she'd been miserable ever since that horrid morning. Wanting to drive him out of her mind, she'd thrown herself into her work, stopping only when absolutely necessary for food or sleep.

Sleep tormented with vivid, hot, sexual dreams that left her sheets tangled and her body aching with unsatisfied hungers that had nothing to do with food. Needless to say, Alec had starred in every one of those dreams.

Her insistence that her obvious weight loss was nothing more than normal female monthly changes had Alec wondering what would have happened if he'd gotten her pregnant that night. Although they'd used protection—well, almost every time, he amended, thinking of that last time in the shower, when they'd not only risked parenthood, but drowning as well—no birth-control method was one-hundred-percent effective.

At the time, he'd had no desire to father a child. But strangely now, picturing Kate ripe and round with his baby was proving eminently appealing.

"That's probably it," he agreed finally, deciding to let her off the hook. For now. After all, he didn't want to push her so far she'd feel the need to run away. "And you don't have to worry. As I said, the dinner's substantial enough to fill you up, but light enough not to keep you from sleeping."

It was also delicious, she discovered as she devoured the steamed corn tortillas, tender chicken and what she'd already learned was the staple of the Amazonian diet, manioc, a tuberous root that when cooked tasted a lot like sweetened tapioca.

"I can't believe I ate all that," she said, staring in wonder at her empty plate. She'd polished it off like some long-haul trucker.

"Well, at least now I don't have to worry that you've become anorexic in the past eleven-and-a-half months."

She didn't like discussing her body with Alec. Not that she really cared what he thought of her.

*Liar.*

"Shut up," she muttered back at her scold. "When I want your opinion, I'll ask for it."

K.J. hadn't even realized that she'd spoken out loud until Alec arched one dark brow.

"Oh, damn." She covered her face with her hands and waited for some smart-ass reply. When none was forthcoming, when the silence stretched so tightly between them she thought her nerves were going to snap, she spread her fingers and peeked up at him. "I suppose you're going to want an explanation."

A corner of his mouth twitched, making K.J. think that if he dared laugh at her, she'd have to slug him. Or cry. Or perhaps she might do both.

"Only if that less-than-cordial statement was directed at me," he said mildly.

"It wasn't." She lowered her arms to the table with a long weary sigh. "You're going to think I'm crazy—"

"I already know you are."

"But…" Embarrassed as she was, it took a moment for his quiet words to sink in. When they did, she stopped and stared at him. "What did you say?"

"I said, I already know you're nuts. Only a crazy woman would leave a comfortable world of trendy restaurants, theaters and art galleries to ride down the Amazon during the rainy season, fight off clouds of mosquitoes and biting flies and eat roots and caiman."

"I didn't have all that much of a choice, if I wanted... Eat what?"

"Caiman. It's a local species of alligator."

"Alligator?" Her eyes dropped to her empty plate. "I thought it was chicken."

He shrugged. "You know what they say—"

"That's frog legs that supposedly taste like chicken," she said, finishing his expected comment.

"Well then, if it helps, just think of your dinner as having been frog legs."

"I've never liked frog legs."

"But you liked the caiman. So, see, you're undoubtedly more adventurous than you thought."

Because his smiling eyes held genuine affection, K.J. smiled back. Just a little. "And crazy." Like her mother, she thought. And her father.

Seeing her father's photographs again after all these years had K.J. remembering, albeit sketchily, those adventurous days when she'd been home-schooled and the entire world had served as both home and school. When she'd arrived at the Campbell estate, Helen Campbell had locked her granddaughter's spirit away into a box, shut the lid and sealed it down tight.

Emotions were dangerous, her grandmother had constantly told her. They weakened propriety, undermined common sense; they made people do foolish things, like risking their lives on glaciated mountaintops and orphaning their child. K.J. had done her best to believe all that. She'd truly tried to keep her feelings stuffed inside that tightly sealed box.

But then she'd met Alec, who'd instantly broken that seal, and once the lid was open, her spirit, and all her emotions, including passions K.J. had never suspected she possessed, had burst free. And now she was beginning to understand the lesson Pandora had learned. That once freed, there could be no locking them away again.

"I suppose it's lucky for both of us that crazy people are my favorite kind," Alec said with a smile that warmed all the cockles of her heart.

This time the silence that settled over them wasn't at all unnerving. In fact, it was actually comfortable, causing K.J. to wonder, yet again, perhaps, if she and Alec both were willing to take the time to get to know one another...

*You don't have that much time. Not if you're going to get the man on the auction block.*

K.J. hated it when her scold was right.

She studied her hands for a long, silent moment, trying to choose her words carefully, which was difficult when her brain was flooded with so many hormones it was all she could do not to leap on the man.

Finally, she lifted her gaze to his patiently waiting one. "I have this...uh, voice," she began slowly, tentatively. She'd never told anyone about the nag. It was too personal. She'd also feared that if she had admitted to hearing voices, she'd end up in a padded room. "In my head."

"Only one?"

His casual tone had her staring at him. "Isn't that enough? I mean, I don't really have any desire to play the starring role in an Amazonian little theater production of *All About Eve*."

"Sounds normal enough to me."

She looked at him harder, seeking the joke at her expense. When she couldn't see it, she decided to go for broke. "That's not all. I talk back to this voice. Sometimes out loud."

*Great tactic. Talk about running the guy off. Of course, it could work to your benefit. Now that he knows about us, he'll rush to sign the divorce papers.*

*Shut up,* she said again, this time managing to keep her response in her head.

"Hey, makes sense to me," Alec said. "Sometimes hearing your thoughts out loud helps clarify things. Especially when you need a sounding board."

"You're not listening, Alec." For some reason she wasn't about to try to figure out, it was imperative that he understand exactly what type of crazy woman he was dealing with. "I don't use the voice as some sort of sounding board. Just the opposite. It's a horribly negative, pessimistic scold who's constantly nagging at me. I don't like it, I don't like its stupidly rigid advice, and most of the time I end up arguing with it."

"What about the other times?"

"What other times?"

"You said most of the time you argue with it. What about those other times?"

"Oh. Then I just shut it off and refuse to listen."

"Again, that sounds perfectly reasonable to me." He studied her silently for a moment. "So, what did it say that night? About me?"

"That I'd be crazy to run off with you."

"But you ignored it."

It was not a question, but K.J. answered it anyway. "Yes. I did."

Again, he didn't answer immediately. Just looked at her with those shrewd gray eyes she suspected never missed a thing.

"I'm glad. Because whatever happens between us, I wouldn't trade that night for anything."

Her eyes stung with traitorous tears, but she was too stubborn to allow a single one to fall. "About that…"

*Remember, you can't afford to antagonize him.*

Once again, she and the scold were in perfect agreement. K.J. swallowed past the lump in her throat, but the words wouldn't come.

All she could do was stare at him, at his shaggy black hair her fingers yearned to comb their way through, at the hard-planed warrior's face she wanted to frame between her palms, at his body—all hard muscle and sinewy strength that she wanted to feel against hers. On top of hers. Inside her.

Hell. The way she was looking at him, the gilded invitation her remarkable eyes were handing him, was all it took to make Alec hard. The steamy air had suddenly turned hot enough to set it boiling around them.

Didn't she realize how vulnerable she was? Alec thought furiously. Didn't she understand that she could stubbornly claim that their marriage was a mistake until doomsday, but if he wanted to drag her out of that chair, throw her onto the hammock—or the dirt floor, for that matter—and take her hard and fast and rough, there wouldn't be a single thing she could do about it?

The civilized world might be coming to the realization that a man could, indeed, be guilty of raping his wife. But they were a very long way from civilization and, with the exception of Rafael, Alec suspected that there wasn't a man in the village, or very many women, who'd hold it against him if he just claimed his husbandly rights and took what he wanted from Kate. What he'd been aching for all these months.

Disgusted with himself when he was actually tempted to do exactly that—because she wouldn't really fight him, he knew—Alec forced down the hunger and reluctantly concentrated on the plan.

"I spent the time while you were asleep thinking about what you said."

As his heated gaze had set her skin to sizzling with sexual awareness, K.J. literally held her breath, waiting for his next move. The one thing she hadn't expected was for the flames in his eyes to be banked and his rough, sexy voice to turn almost remote.

"About what?" Her own voice, thin and needy, was that of a stranger.

"About our marriage being a sham."

He picked up her left hand from the table, seeming entranced with the bare fourth finger. The one he'd slipped that gold ring on. The very same ring she'd left behind in the hotel room, along, with her heart, she'd belatedly discovered.

"Oh?" It was part whisper, part croak.

"I was thinking that you may be right."

"I see." Unfortunately, she did. All too clearly. She took a deep breath and tried to ignore the surprising pain that felt like a dagger through her heart. "Well, then, I suppose it's time for me to tell you the entire story about why I've come here."

Alec didn't say a single word as she explained all about the bachelor auction, how his name had unexpectedly come up, how she'd felt pushed into a corner. And, most importantly, how the auction was for such a worthwhile cause. Once she'd started, the words poured out, like water over a dam.

"All right," Alec said when she'd finally run down.

K.J. stared at him, looking for the catch. "Then you'll do it?"

"If it'll help you out."

"Oh, it will." Why didn't she feel relief? she wondered. "And literacy is so important—"

"I already contribute to literacy, Kate. The only reason I'm agreeing is because you seem to believe your career depends on me making a fool of myself."

"You could never look foolish, Alec," she said earnestly. "And you'll see, it might even be fun, having a roomful of women fighting over you."

There was only one woman Alec wanted. And she was sitting right here, close enough that he could smell the herbal shampoo that reminded him of an alpine meadow.

"I'm not certain what the procedures are for getting a divorce in this country," he continued, seemingly unaware of what remained of her heart lying in tatters all around them on the hard-packed earthen floor. "But we can ask Rafael in the morning. He might know. Since he also has several friends in the government, he should be able to grease a few wheels to arrange a divorce, or annulment, or whatever is faster to obtain."

Although she'd always thought herself a courageous woman, K.J. found she could not meet Alec's gaze. Not when she feared that the hot moist sheen filling her eyes would give away her tumultuous thoughts. "If that's what you want," she said quietly.

"I didn't when you first arrived this afternoon. But it's what you want. Isn't it?"

Here was her out, K.J. told herself. She should just tell him the truth before she got into this ridiculous lie too deeply. She should admit that what she really wanted to do was rip his shirt off his body and press her face against his chest. She longed to taste the tangy flavor of his flesh, drink in his musky male scent, feel the ridges of rippling muscle beneath her fingertips.

But that wouldn't be nearly enough. Then she wanted to tear open those faded jeans and release his thick, heavy sex, and cup it in her hands, stroke it with her fingernails and tongue, take it deep into her mouth....

No! K.J. had to remind herself that she'd come all this way on a mission, not to jump into bed with the most perfect specimen of a male she'd ever met, a man who'd make any romance cover model look like a wimp and any fictional romantic hero seem like a piker. As thrilling as it would be, a sexual encounter with Alec would only complicate matters because, unfortunately, there was no future in it.

Her life was not here in the godforsaken jungle. She'd plotted her future carefully, since her grandmother had first insisted that if K.J. was determined to become a photographer, she should at least have the good sense to have a career to fall back on.

Somehow, when she hadn't been paying enough attention, her editing had taken precedence over her photography. But that would surely change once she earned her promotion and had more time, more breathing room.

Her path was laid out before her, and while it might not exactly be a yellow brick road, and it certainly wasn't leading to anything as magical as Oz, K.J. realized, even on the bad days, that it was a lot better than most people's.

And although Alec had, admittedly, been a stimulating detour on that previously straight and narrow path, it was now time to continue on.

She briefly closed her eyes against the pain caused by that decision, then resolutely opened them and forced her gaze back up to his.

"Yes," she finally answered him. The ragged whisper was barely audible even in the close confines of the hut. It was also less than convincing. She cleared her throat, then tried again. "A divorce is what I want."

"You wouldn't lie to me, would you, Kate? Not about a thing as important as this?"

"No," she lied through her teeth.

K.J. thought she saw a flicker of disappointment in his slate gray eyes, but it came and went so quickly, she couldn't be certain.

"Fine." The single word was clipped and as final as the deadly thud of an executioner's ax. "Now that we've gotten that settled, I guess I'll be going, since I have to leave the village early tomorrow morning and—"

"You're leaving?"

Alec viewed the panic in her eyes, watched the color drain from her sunburned face. He wondered whether his wife was actually distraught at the idea of being separated again, or if she was merely afraid his departure would interfere with her divorce.

"I'll only be gone for the day. I'm going a couple of miles upriver, but I'll be back in plenty of time to escort you to the festival."

Eloping with Alec had been a rash act, and chasing him down here to the Amazon had definitely been reckless, but feeling the way she did—like a hot, seething, tempestuous Vesuvius about to blow—K.J. decided that attending a fertility pageant with this man would be, hands down, the most dangerous thing she'd ever done.

"I'm still not certain that's a very good idea."

"You don't want to miss the opportunity for some once-in-a-lifetime shots," he said again. "Shots you'd never get back home in the city. Besides, I don't see how we can avoid it. Since everyone in the village knows we're married—"

"They do?"

"Word travels faster than you'd think down here," he said. "And since divorce isn't really a concept in their tribal social structure, now that you've finally arrived, it would seem strange—and rude—if I showed up in public without you."

Since it appeared she was going to be stuck here for at least the next couple of days, K.J. definitely didn't want to insult her hosts. Or cause Alec any unnecessary embarrassment.

"All right. Since you put it that way." Another thought occurred to her. "If they know we're married—technically—won't they think it strange that you're spending the night with Rafael?"

This time she knew she didn't imagine the flames that sparked in his silver-gray eyes. "Are you inviting me to stay here? With you?"

"Not in any…uh, intimate way…but I suppose we could work out some arrangement. I certainly wouldn't want to damage your reputation with the tribe."

"You needn't concern yourself with that. To tell the truth, it's your reputation you should be worrying about."

"Mine?"

"In this culture, a woman who can't keep a husband in her bed is looked upon as pretty much a failure."

*He's challenging you, trying to bring the subject back to sex. Whatever you do, don't fall into his trap and remind him that you certainly didn't have any problem keeping him in bed the night of your honeymoon.*

Feminine pride flared as K.J. ignored the harpy and

lifted her chin in a challenge of her own. "I could have you on your knees."

"Absolutely," he agreed instantly. "Willingly. Gladly. In fact, now that you bring it up, remember how—"

"I remember," she snapped, cutting him off before he reminded her of how he'd slowly rolled down her stockings, one at a time, then licked his wicked way back up her legs, tormenting with his teeth and tongue until she'd come to pieces standing there beside the bed, before they'd even gotten around to taking off the rest of their clothes.

Once again, she managed, just barely, to force her raging hormones back into their steel cage. "What about the husband?" she asked, "Isn't he expected to keep up his part? So to speak?"

"Sure. In fact, the survival of the tribe depends on his ability to perform. Since this is a matriarchal society, the women pretty much call the shots, which is why it's considered normal courting behavior to have a sexual rehearsal the week before the wedding."

"Rehearsal?"

"Yeah. The couple disappear into the bridal hut and don't come out until the morning of the ceremony. Foods believed to be aphrodisiacs are placed in front of the door, to increase libido and keep their strength up. And each night the rest of the tribe chants to the gods for the union to be a success. I've always thought it wasn't such a bad way for the woman to try out a prospective groom before the wedding. Just to make certain everything's in working order."

His grin was quick and wickedly seductive in a way that caused K.J.'s blood to spike. It also reminded her that everything about Alec had been in splendid working order.

"But after marriage, things even out a bit and it's up to both of them to keep things interesting," he continued. "I hear some of the techniques are very innovative. In fact, if even half of the stories I've heard are remotely true, Masters and Johnson would probably have a field day studying these people's sexual behavior."

Just talking about sex with this man had K.J. feeling on the verge of meltdown. Although the afternoon thunderstorm had passed, enough electricity was sparking between them to supply power to this village for at least a year.

"Speaking of bed," she murmured, stifling a fake yawn as she tried to ignore the throbbing between her legs. "I think perhaps it's time I went to sleep. Despite my nap, I'm still tired, and since you said you have to leave early in the morning…"

"Good point." He pushed himself up from the table and stood over her. "I put a pitcher of fresh water, a cup and a bowl on the chest, just in case you didn't want to go back outside in the dark."

He pointed at the piece of bamboo furniture on a far wall. Pitcher, bowl and cup were obviously handmade from clay and, taking in the intricate designs of local animals and plant life, K.J. knew that more than one New York gallery would love to represent the artisan.

"There's also some cream for your face. To ease the sunburn. So—" he shrugged "—I guess that's about it. Unless you need anything else?"

"No." *Other than desperately wanting you to make mad, passionate love to me all night long, I'm just dandy,* she thought. "I'll be fine."

Another lie. Beads of perspiration glistened on that dark triangle of tanned male flesh framed by the open collar of his shirt; K.J. found herself nearly overcome with the desire to lick them off.

As if reading her unruly mind, Alec reached down, caught her chin in his fingers and treated her to a hard quick kiss that, even as brief as it was, would have knocked her off her feet if she hadn't already been sitting down.

Even after he'd lifted his head, he didn't release her. He continued to tower over her, his serious expression causing her breath to clog in her lungs.

Just when she thought he was going to say something, he took his hands away and jammed them deep into his front pockets, drawing her gaze to where the denim was pulling tight against the unmistakable bulge that, heaven help her, seemed to be growing bigger as she watched.

"See anything you like?" he asked.

"What?" K.J. guiltily dragged her eyes back up to his face.

"You were staring, Mrs. Mackenzie." His deep voice rumbled like distant thunder.

"I was not."

"Were too." He murmured the childhood playground taunt, although they both knew that the game they were playing was definitely rated Adults Only. "As I said, this is a matriarchal society, Kate. So anytime you want your husband to scratch that itch that's obviously bedeviling the hell out of you, sweetheart, just whistle."

He flashed her his wickedest, most seductive grin yet, then walked out with a loose-hipped male stride that could only be described as a swagger.

As he closed the door, which was fashioned from tree limbs behind him, K.J.'s breath finally escaped her lungs with a huge whoosh.

She lowered her forehead to the table and closed her eyes, squeezing off the hot tears that threatened once again.

"What in the world am I going to do?" she moaned.

For once, her pessimistic scold, always so quick to offer advice, remained absolutely silent.

# 10

As EXHAUSTED AS SHE WAS, K.J. found sleep an impossible target. She would have expected the night to be far less noisy than back in the city. After all, the jungle was less populated; there wouldn't be the unceasing drone of traffic outside her window, punctuated by angry blasts of car horns, loud drunken arguments and the scream of sirens coming from the fire station across the street. But she hadn't counted on the fact that the jungle had its own inhabitants, and while she might have gotten used to the trumpeting of horns from the parade of trucks carrying the early edition of the *New York Times* to newsstands all over the city, the cacophony of Amazonian night sounds was both constant and a little frightening.

First there were the whistles, whoops and cackles of birds settling down in the tops of the towering trees. These eventually, for the most part, drifted off, only to be replaced by the deep croak of frogs, the occasional plaintive cries of a baby from somewhere in the village, the snorts and grunts of some nearby animal, the screeches of monkeys that sounded much like a person being tortured.

Although it was not K.J.'s first night in the jungle, it was her first alone after encountering the one man she feared was even more dangerous than any wild animal. Adrenaline was coursing through her veins, and whenever she tried to take her mind off the eerie sounds, it would jump immediately to Alec, reliving every moment of the day, every word of conversation, every lingering kiss, every caressing touch, every hot look, like an unending videotape in her head.

K.J. was accustomed to living alone. But never, except for those first few nights after she'd left Las Vegas, had she ever felt so lonely. She tossed and turned, causing the hammock to sway like a paper boat caught in a riptide.

Although the sun had gone down hours ago, the air hadn't cooled. And that afternoon rain, as always, had only made things worse. The cotton nightshirt she'd changed into after Alec had left was already damp and clung uncomfortably to her hot clammy skin. She thought about stripping it off, but the idea of being naked in this dark and foreign place made her feel too vulnerable. So she continued to suffer in silence.

Unfortunately, her scold wasn't so stoic. *This is what you get*, it complained, *bringing us down to this godforsaken place. And for what? An outside chance of dragging your husband back to the city?*

"He's already agreed to a divorce." It was what she wanted. One of the two things she'd come all this way for. So why did his rapid capitulation have her feeling so depressed?

*He agreed to have his friend look into a divorce. That's not exactly the same thing. How do you know he isn't pretending to go along with your request in order to keep you here with him as long as he can?*

"Alec would never do that." Although she might be confused about a great many things, including her tempestuous, mercurial feelings, of this K.J. was absolutely certain. "He's unrelentingly honest. And outspoken."

He'd looked deep into her eyes that moment he'd

taken hold of her hand in the Round Table Banquet Hall and told her, in a husky voice that vibrated through her bones: "You're the most beautiful woman in this room, and I want you." How much more outspoken could he be?

"He'd never lie to me," K.J. said firmly. "And he's not that sneaky."

*A man will do whatever it takes to get a woman into his bed. If that means resorting to lies and trickery, he won't hesitate.*

"Have I ever mentioned that you could use a serious attitude adjustment?" K.J. grunted between clenched teeth.

*One of us has to remain sensible. Since your brain seems to turn to mush whenever you're anywhere near that man.*

K.J. sighed. She didn't argue this salient point. There was, after all, no need. Since it was regrettably true.

Sometime much, much later, she finally dozed off into a restless sleep plagued by dreams that would definitely have been slapped with an *X* rating by any media-ratings review board back home. But eventually, she gradually became aware that the heavy pressure in her lower regions was not due solely to raging hormones, but another call of nature every bit as strong.

She turned on the propane lantern beside the bed and looked down at her watch. "Aw, damn!" It was only two in the morning. There was no way she was going to make it to daybreak, which meant that she was going to have to make that short walk through the dark by herself.

Surrendering to the inevitable, she pushed the mosquito netting aside and dragged her weary bones out of the hammock. She pulled on her hiking boots—after first shaking them out to make certain that no insects or snakes had decided to use them for a motel for the night. Since she wasn't going all that far, she didn't bother to tie the laces. Then, picking up the lantern and grabbing a handful of tissues, she took a deep breath, as if the amount of bravery she possessed was in direct proportion to the oxygen in her lungs, then opened the door.

The jungle night was as black as pitch, filled with shifting shadows K.J. assured herself were only leaves and palm fronds swaying in the breeze. For the sake of sanity, she ignored the fact that the thick, moist night air was as still as a tomb. Something skittered through the decaying leaves at her feet.

Jumping backward, she put one hand up to her mouth to stifle her scream, using the other to hold up the lantern. The spreading yellow glow revealed a small colorful snake slithering away into the shadows.

*Your cockeyed plan is going to get us killed!* The panic in the scold's voice echoed K.J.'s own and was barely discernible over the pounding of the blood in her ears.

"He was probably as frightened by me as I was him," K.J. replied, trying to reassure them both. In her case, she failed miserably. "After all, he was a lot smaller."

*So's a vampire bat.*

K.J. merely shook her head, watching where she walked even more carefully as she continued on to the outhouse. She hurried as fast as she could, and was on her way back to the hut when a low sound somewhere between a distant roll of thunder and a cat's purr had her stopping dead in her tracks.

*Don't stop! Run!*

"Shut up, dammit," she hissed as she gingerly lifted the lantern higher, above her head, and looked in the direction of the faint sound. It was, unfortunately, between where she was standing and the hut.

She heard it again. At the same time she viewed a pair of eyes gleaming like yellow diamonds in the ebony night.

*That's it. We're goners. I certainly hope you're satisfied now, girl.*

There had to be a way out of this, K.J. thought, her head spinning wildly. Unfortunately, it was the only thing working, since her booted feet seemed to be stuck in quicksand and her body, like Job's wife, had turned to a block of salt.

This time the throaty sound was unmistakably more growl than purr. As the jaguar moved out of the shadows toward her, K.J.'s feet suddenly obeyed her command to take off running. Unfortunately, her head forgot that it would be safer to run toward the village, rather than deeper into the dense black jungle.

When she stubbed her left foot on the exposed root of a tree, she began to fall. If her boots had been tied, she might have managed to keep running, but the laces tangled, sending her sprawling. Her scream echoed through the night, causing a noisy exodus of birds from the tops of the trees.

As if having a wild killer cat stalking you wasn't bad enough, when she felt strong hands plucking her from the ground, she opened her mouth to call out for help, but her cry was smothered by the hard wall of the chest she was suddenly being smashed against.

"It's okay. Don't worry, sweetheart. He's gone. You're safe."

Through her wildly whirling senses, K.J. recognized the wonderfully familiar voice. "Oh, Alec!" Despite the fact that he was holding her tight enough to practically squeeze the last bit of air from her lungs, she managed to fling her arms around his neck and cling. "I...was..." she gulped for breath "...so f-f-frightened."

"I know," he soothed. Those same hands that had snatched her from the clutches of sure death were stroking her back, the caresses meant to calm rather than seduce. "But you don't have to worry." His cheek was pressed against the top of her head, his breath a warm, but oh, so welcome, breeze against her pounding temple. "I'd never let anything happen to you."

And because it was Alec saying it, K.J. believed him absolutely.

She lifted a hand to his face. At the same time, a dark cloud drifted across the night sky, revealing a crescent of moon. The silvery stream of light illuminated his face, allowing her to see the way his eyes had darkened again to that thrilling, terrifying, stormy-sea hue. A muscle along his sharply chiseled cheekbone jerked beneath her tingling fingertips.

She didn't beg. As she looked up at Alec and he looked down at her, they both knew there was no need.

He let out a pent-up breath, then, in one violent motion, yanked her against him. Feeling his rock-hard arousal, knowing that she'd caused that dramatic response, fanned the flames of her own desire even higher, and this time her soft cry was one of wonder. Of need.

As his mouth closed over hers, not gently, Alec was consumed with urgency. He forgot gentleness, surrendered control to the wild warrior within as he plundered, taking what he wanted and demanding more.

He'd gone from merely tasting to devouring in a single rapid-fire heartbeat. His hands were everywhere, cruising over her face, tangling in her hair, diving below the thigh-length cotton nightshirt to race over her body with an incendiary touch that turned her blood to thick rivers of flame and scorched away any thought of resistance.

She was burning up. Heat was radiating from her pores. Her flesh, wherever Alec's wonderfully wicked hands touched, burned. With her mind engulfed in billowing smoke that clouded all reason, with every ounce of restraint seared away, K.J. pressed herself against him, rotating her hips with blatant female hunger.

For a man who'd always prided himself on his control, Alec was discovering yet again that restraint was absolutely impossible whenever he was with this woman. The ragged, desperately needy sounds that were torn from her smooth white throat sent desire ripping through him like a buzz saw. The feel of her yielding body against his throbbing one, the need to reclaim every curve and hollow were enough to make him mad with lust.

Memories flooded his head, his blood, his loins. He had no doubt that he could take her now, hard and fast in a whirlwind of passion that would temporarily ease all the pent-up desire that had been arcing between them from the first.

But then what? Alec was forced to wonder as a clap of thunder directly overhead literally shook the ground. A flash of sulfurous lightning followed, and although this afternoon's storm had passed, the sky suddenly opened up, drenching them with warm, stinging needles of rain.

Needing to back away from the edge of the dangerous cliffs before he went tumbling headfirst into oblivion, Alec dragged his mouth from her sweet, eager lips and pressed it against the top of her head.

"Lord, I'm glad you're finally here." He didn't bother to censure his words when his body, his hunger, had already given her insight to feelings he usually kept guarded. Unable to give up touching her quite yet, he moved his hands up and down her torso beneath the now-soaked nightshirt, caressing her in a way that teased and stimulated them both. "There were times when I thought I'd go stark raving mad waiting for you to show up."

"I felt the same way," she gasped as his clever, knowing fingers tugged on a turgid nipple. The rain was pouring down her upturned face, dripping from his dark wet hair, but neither of them paid it any heed.

"Yet you insisted on staying away."

"You could have come to me," she reminded him. And herself. All right, she may have been the one to run away, but she wasn't the only one who'd turned her back on their marriage.

"I told you, dammit, that I had planned this expedition for months. Years."

She pulled a little away from him. "I also remember you saying that it was more important than a quickie unplanned marriage."

His curse was rich, ripe and too harsh to ever be allowed on the pages of any Heart romance novel. "Dammit, we've come full circle." He swiped his hand furiously through his hair, shaking water from his head like a dog after a bath. "We're back to the question of which means more to me—my work or you."

"I'd say that question's already been answered. It's more than obvious which you care more about."

"That's a pretty quick assumption for a woman

who's already admitted she doesn't know me all that well."

He was towering over her in a way meant to intimidate, but K.J. held her ground. "I might not be acquainted with the little details of your life before we met, Alec. But I certainly know where I stand in your personal hierarchy."

He glared down at her, his eyes so hot K.J. was vaguely surprised that he hadn't turned the rain streaming down both their faces to steam. He'd taken his hands from beneath her nightshirt and had curled them into fists at his sides.

*Now you've done it. He's going to hit us.*

"You'd never hit me," she assured them all—herself, her scold and, just in the possible event he might be wavering, Alec.

"Want to bet?"

"I may not know you all that well. But I do know you're not the type of man ever to strike a woman."

"Perhaps I've never met one who could make me so damn mad so fast." His fists loosened, but only so his fingers could curl around her shoulders, digging hard into her skin beneath the wet cotton, as if he were considering shaking some sense into her.

He stared at her for another long moment, in a way that made him appear as if he could slash and burn the entire jungle with his eyes.

Then, as abruptly as he'd pulled her into his arms, he released her and picked up the lantern she'd dropped. "You don't know squat, sweetheart."

From the acidic contempt in his gravel-rough voice, K.J. knew he hadn't meant that "sweetheart" as an endearment.

He bent his head until their faces were only inches

apart. "Now, let's get that tight little butt back into the hut before I turn it over my knee."

An intriguing blend of fear and heat flickered through her. "And here I thought you weren't into kinky sex."

His eyes blazed even hotter, but standing this close to him, K.J. thought she saw his lips twitch. "Don't tempt me."

Taking hold of her arm, he dragged her back to the hut and shoved her inside, then turned to leave again.

"Where are you going?" she asked, unable to keep the renewed panic from her voice.

The kiss and the argument had somehow managed to drive the thought of that deadly killer jaguar from her mind. But now it was back with a vengeance, and the truth was that she didn't want to spend the rest of the time until daylight alone.

He looked on the verge of saying something sarcastic, then his expression softened. "All the beer I had today's backing up on me."

"Oh." That explained what he was doing outside when she'd needed to be rescued. Timing, K.J. thought, was indeed everything.

"I'll be right back." His gaze moved over her as it had earlier in the evening, making her all too aware of the way the sodden material was clinging to her breasts and thighs. "And, if you don't want to find out just how kinky I can be," he said gruffly, "I suggest you change into some dry clothes."

With that he was gone, leaving her alone again. But this time, instead of wanting to weep, K.J. wrapped her arms around herself and smiled.

She would not have been smiling if she could have seen the meeting between the two best friends a few yards from the hut.

"Thanks," Alec said.

"Then it worked?" Rafael asked.

"Like a charm." What had, admittedly, been a long shot, had definitely been worth waiting up for.

When the animal beside him growled, Alec reached down and patted the spotted head. The jaguar's low growl turned to purrs, and if animals could smile, this one was pulling it off. Though, due to the complete absence of teeth, the grin was lacking in intensity.

"Good girl," Alec told Rafael's pet jaguar, who began purring all the louder.

"If she finds out you tricked her, your wife will not be a happy woman."

"By the time she finds out, we'll have reconciled, and she'll think me a dashing romance novel hero for using any means at my disposal to win my woman back."

"I hope you're right," Rafael said, his expression less assured than Alec's.

"It'll work," Alec insisted. It had to. Because even in this part of the world, tying Kate up and keeping her prisoner until she relented might be a bit over the top. "Are you ready for part two?"

"Yes, but I still have concerns—"

"It'll work," Alec said again. "I'll see you at the river at first light."

Rafael murmured an agreement, then disappeared back into the shadows, the jaguar following obediently.

As Alec returned to his bride, he couldn't help whistling under his breath. Things, he thought with a strong sense of satisfaction, were definitely beginning to look up.

# 11

A PALE LILAC LIGHT was shimmering through the wicker slats covering the windows when K.J. woke again. She looked down at the floor beside the hammock, where Alec had spent the night alone in his bedroll. He was gone. Although she wanted to just turn over and go back to sleep, she reminded herself that he could always change his mind about giving her the divorce—which why she couldn't allow him to spend the entire day away from the village alone.

After covering herself with sunscreen and insect repellent, she threw on a pair of shorts, T-shirt, her hat and boots, and scooped up her camera bag. She left the hut and, following her instincts, found him down by the river in the same spot where she'd landed yesterday. He was loading a motorboat with what appeared to be electronic equipment.

"Good morning." His greeting was accompanied by a friendly smile. "I didn't expect to see you down here."

"I was thinking I might go with you. To take some photographs. If you don't mind, that is."

"Sure. It'll be nice to have company." He held out a hand to help her aboard. "Perhaps you'll bring me luck."

"I wouldn't count on it." She stepped onto the deck, pleased that it felt much sturdier than yesterday's dugout canoe. "Since my luck hasn't exactly been stellar since I left New York."

"Then it's undoubtedly due for a change."

"I can only hope you're right."

K.J. smiled a greeting at Rafael, who'd just come from belowdecks. "Good morning."

"Good morning to you." His dark eyes were warm with a male appreciation that was in no way threatening. "May I say you look very lovely this morning, Kate?" After she'd murmured her thanks, he asked, "So, I trust you slept well?"

"For the most part." Kate refused to look at Alec. She just knew he'd take the opportunity to remind her, with merely a look, of how she'd literally thrown herself into his arms.

"It is often difficult, sleeping in a strange place," Rafael said.

She thought she heard a note of laughter in his voice and decided that she must be imagining it.

"I asked Rafael about our problem," Alec said. "And, apparently, it's not going to be that hard to dissolve the marriage."

"Is that right?" she asked with a calm that belied the fact that her heart had just sunk to her toes.

"Alec exaggerates a bit. It will not be exactly easy, either," Rafael warned. "It will require an official form signed and notarized by a government official."

"I see." K.J. immediately got his drift. "And I assume there aren't any officials handy in Santa Clara."

"I am afraid not. They're all in the capital city."

"And where is that?"

"About three day's journey downriver. But only a few hours by plane."

"Well, that doesn't sound too bad," she decided. She looked toward Alec, who was busy on the other side of the boat with ropes. "Do you think we could go today?"

"Sorry, sweetheart." Alec shook his head. The dark glasses he was wearing prevented her from seeing his eyes, but she didn't hear a great deal of regret in his voice. "But I've planned today's search for a long time."

"And one day will make that much difference? After all this time?"

"Actually, it will. See, the Global Positioning System works with satellite communications, and as you no doubt learned in science class, they're out there circling the Earth—"

"I know about satellites, Alec."

"Of course you do. But you see, today's the only day all eight of them are perfectly in line."

"And that makes a difference?"

Alec studiously avoided looking toward his friend. "Absolutely," he lied blithely. "I've been waiting months for just this exact alignment, which should give me the optimum positioning to compare the current river basin with my map of the treasure."

"You actually have a treasure map?"

"Of course. I told you all about it that night. It came in an old sea captain's log I ran across in Barcelona."

"A sea captain's treasure map? Are you certain it isn't some prize some kid got with Captain Crunch box tops?"

"Nah." If he was the slightest bit wounded by her sarcasm, Alec didn't show it. "My secret decoder ring came with box tops. This is an authentic log. From a respectable antique bookstore."

"If it's so authentic, why haven't you located the treasure? You've been down here almost a year."

"I know exactly how long I've been here, Kate." His

tone had turned momentarily gruff. "But landscapes change over centuries, especially in this part of the country, where the river is constantly reclaiming land and covering other parts of it up again. And besides, as I said, I'm using satellite imaging, and—"

"This is the first day all eight satellites are in alignment," she said dryly.

"Exactly." He beamed at her like a proud teacher.

"How about tomorrow?" she asked.

"I don't know." He rubbed his chin, which, she noticed, he'd shaved this morning. "It's kind of a forty-eight-hour window we're working with."

"They stay in alignment for two whole days?"

"They're slow-moving satellites. Comparatively speaking, of course."

"Of course."

She suspected he was lying, but had no way to prove it. K.J. now wished she'd paid more attention during her junior high science classes.

"How about the day after tomorrow, then?"

He sighed and shook his head. "You're definitely a Campbell, Kate. I doubt I've ever met a more stubborn woman."

"And I've never met a more frustrating man." Her hands were on her waist, her chin pointed straight at him. "Last night you agreed that a divorce was the best solution."

"Because that's what you wanted."

"Well, nothing's changed since then."

"Nothing?" He lifted a brow, reminding her of that hot, hungry kiss they'd shared when he'd rescued her from the killer jaguar.

K.J. refused to be intimidated. "Nothing important."

It was not a lie. Nothing had changed. He could still

make her ache with a single look, a caressing touch; he was still determined to find his stupid Inca gold; he still possessed the power to break her heart. And she still needed to bring a bachelor back to New York.

As they stood there, like two children engaged in a staring contest in a playground, K.J. asked herself what she'd do if Alec was suddenly willing to give up his treasure hunt. If he'd promise to put her first in his life.

That question had her reluctantly admitting that she wasn't exactly being fair. Would she do the same? she asked herself. Would she risk being fired by returning to New York without him? Or, even more recklessly, would she turn her back on the security of her editorial job, and all its accompanying benefits, and stay down here in the jungle to help him find his treasure?

When she realized that they'd probably been at cross purposes from the beginning, she bit her lip and turned away, back toward Rafael, who'd wisely stayed out of the conversation.

"I suppose this paper has to be signed by both people in the presence of the official."

"Yes." His eyes offered sympathy.

"Well, then." She seemed to have come to a dead end. Although Alec might be willing to grant her a divorce, he wasn't willing to lift a finger to help her get one.

Frustrated, she was trying to decide whether to curse or cry when Alec surprised her yet again by putting down the rope he'd been coiling.

"I'll make you a deal."

"What?"

"Give me three more days."

"To find the treasure?"

"That, too." His lips quirked in a ghost of a smile. "Then, if you still want a divorce—"

"I will."

"If you still want a divorce," he repeated doggedly, "I'll take you to the capital, sign the paper and return to New York with you for that damn auction. Then afterward, we can go our separate ways."

She'd already determined that it was important to listen carefully to this man. Even taking away the chemical brain bath she'd been experiencing that night, K.J. realized that there were unspoken nuances underlying so many of his statements. Although she'd thought him outspoken, she was beginning to understand that it was every bit as important to listen to what he wasn't saying.

"Do you promise?"

"I swear on the family Bible Ian Mackenzie brought with him from Scotland." Alec lifted his right hand in a pledge.

"I don't see any Bible."

"Fine." He huffed a frustrated breath. "How about I swear on the honor of the Mackenzie name?"

She crossed her arms, and although she wasn't in a much better position than five minutes ago, K.J. was almost enjoying herself. "Now there's something I can trust." Her dry tone said otherwise.

He put a hand over his chest. "You wound me, Kate."

The masculine irritation in his eyes had softened to something far more dangerous. As she felt herself being drawn into that silver snare, K.J. struggled to remind herself how vital it was to stick to the plan.

She lifted her hand to rub the back of her neck, where the tension had settled. "Didn't you say something about not wanting to waste this valuable window of time waiting for the satellites to become aligned?"

He couldn't help smiling at the way she'd turned businesslike on him. It reminded him of that gray suit she'd worn to dinner; both were protective camouflage.

"Good point." He turned toward Rafael. "Good luck with the preparations for the festival. We'll see you this evening."

"I'll be watching for you." Rafael held a small book toward Kate. "Occasionally, days on the river can seem exceedingly long, even when you have things to do, such as taking your pictures," he said. "I thought you might enjoy this to read in your spare time."

The paper was thinner than she was used to and the cover lacked the book-rack appeal necessary to get readers to stop and take a look. But the name on the cover was definitely familiar. "You wrote this?"

"Actually, I served more as editor, simply writing down the old tribal legends that have been passed down orally through the generations."

She smiled. "I'm definitely looking forward to reading it. Thank you."

"It's my pleasure. Adios, Kate. Until tonight." His bow would have been appropriate in a fifteenth century Spanish court. Kate found it charming. Alec looked irritated.

Neither spoke as they watched him walk away. When he'd disappeared into the crowd of villagers who'd come out of their thatched huts to begin their day, Alec turned toward K.J.

"Ready to cast off?"

The thought of being alone with him all day did not seem quite as simple as it had when she'd first awakened. K.J. assured herself that Alec was not the kind of man who'd force himself on a woman. She also reminded herself that if she wanted a divorce—and she did—she was going to have to keep her distance from him today. Both physically and emotionally.

*That's going to be difficult. On such a small boat.*

K.J. really hated it when her scold stated the obvious. She straightened her back and her resolve.

"Ready," she said, tamping down the uneasy feeling that she'd just agreed to go skydiving—without a parachute.

K.J. spent the first hour standing at the rail of the boat, snapping shot after shot: photographs of women beating clothing against rocks, children bathing at the edge of the river, men spearing huge fish that glittered like silver in the early morning sunlight, long-legged herons wading along the muddy bank, crayon-hued macaws flying overhead and clouds of huge butterflies that fluttered through the moisture laden air, their wings glistening in the bright Amazon sun like precious jewels.

As the sun rose higher in the sky, she felt its heat on her face—which was much better today, thanks to whatever fragrant balm Alec had given her—and moved beneath the canvas awning. Since this wasn't exactly a pleasure craft, it didn't have any lounge chairs, but she was content to sit cross-legged on the reed mat on deck and watch the scenery. And her husband.

He'd turned down a tributary thirty minutes earlier, and although she had no idea where they were, K.J. had decided to put her trust in Alec's G.P.S. system and the perfectly aligned satellites.

Rather than the muddy brown color of the wider Amazon, this smaller river was a satin ribbon as blue as the sky above them. It also ran through a slot canyon that had K.J. feeling extremely grateful that she wasn't claustrophobic.

The motor hummed as they followed the narrowing tributary upstream. It was the only sound in the cathedral-like silence surrounding them, a quiet beauty only untamed nature could produce. K.J. hadn't seen another person since they'd turned off from the main river.

She watched Alec thread the boat through the reeds and the narrow passage with a skill that she suspected could never be taught. For not the first time since she'd arrived in Santa Clara, she thought how he seemed to be in his element in this remote and wild land.

"I just realized what this reminds me of," she said as they approached their third hour on the river.

"What?"

"*The African Queen.*"

"This isn't Africa."

"Well, of course I know that. But it's a great deal the same. A wild, foreign river, a desolate place—"

"A man and a woman who could be the only two people in the world," he said. The reeds were beginning to grow thicker. Alec checked his depth finder to ensure they wouldn't run aground.

"That, too," she admitted.

Alec found himself rather liking that idea. "So, do you see me as Humphrey Bogart?"

"Absolutely."

He liked that, too.

"Do you see me as Katharine Hepburn?" The canyon was now narrow enough that if she'd wanted to, K.J. could have stretched her arms out and touched both towering rock walls.

"Nah."

"Oh." Her voice held a faint tinge of disappointment.

"You're a lot prettier. And a lot more fun than she was in the early part of that movie."

"She'd been raised to be a proper lady. Her upbringing hadn't included any preparation for river running with a belching, swearing, hard-drinking man like Charles Allnutt."

The grin Alec flashed her was pure Bogie. "Sounds like some other Kate I know. Perhaps the two of you have more in common than I first thought." He gave it a bit more consideration as he slowed the engine. The tangled greenery was definitely beginning to remind him too much of that classic movie. "You both have spunk."

Spunk. K.J. liked that. Liked that he thought it of her even more. "Charlie respected her for that."

"And even reluctantly came to like her," Alec agreed. "By the time they'd gotten past the leeches, he knew he was sunk."

"Is that how you see being in love?" she asked, honestly curious. "As being sunk?"

There was a brief silence as he thought her question over. "Not if it's reciprocated, as it was in their case."

He cursed as they suddenly emerged from the narrow canyon upon a lake that was almost entirely green with water plants. The roots of the plants and the trees had matted together to form islands of vegetation.

The lake reminded K.J. of a wild botanical garden. Branches bent low beneath the weight of passion fruit vines; the vine roots tangled with pale moss that hung down like uncombed hair. Clumps of bright flowers, their petals flared like trumpets, rose out of the thick greenery like oversize bouquets; bees as big as hummingbirds buzzed from bright blossom to blossom. In the distance, far across the lake, she could see the shadowy purple form of a mountain. If she closed one eye and squinted just right, its craggy form somewhat resembled a sleeping giant.

"What now?" K.J. asked quietly, sensing Alec's frustration.

"I don't know." He raked his hand through his hair. "I thought for certain this was the canyon—it matches all the writings in the log. But there was nothing about a lake."

"You said yourself that the riverbed is always changing."

"True. But certain landmarks should stay the same. Even a river as wide and wild as the Amazon can't completely wash away an entire mountain. Not even in five hundred years."

He glared out across the lake, then down at the screen of his ultrasonic device, which kept him apprised of the depth of the water, then up at the sky, where the daily, gray-bordered clouds were already beginning to gather.

"And wouldn't you know it." His growl reminded K.J. a great deal of last night's jaguar. "The damn rain's going to start early."

"I'm sorry."

"Hell, you didn't do anything."

"Well, of course I didn't. But you were hoping I'd change your luck, and——"

"People make their own luck," he said, unknowingly echoing what her grandmother Campbell had said on more than one occasion while K.J. had been growing up. He ripped off his tattered Seattle Mariners baseball cap and dragged his fingers through his shaggy dark hair. "They're also pretty much responsible for their own fate. Which means we're going to have to turn back."

"So soon?"

"It's not exactly my choice either, Kate. But if we're in that canyon when the rains hit, we could be in a major world of hurt."

She remembered the rapids she'd survived yesterday, just before arriving at the village. Recalled all too well how she'd been positive she was going to die. The idea of being locked into the towering canyon with so much wild churning water was definitely unappealing.

"I'm sorry," she said again, hating the frustration she saw in his eyes.

"Yeah." He slammed the cap back onto his head. "Me, too."

Since he didn't seem to be inclined toward conversation, K.J. spent most of the way back to Santa Clara immersed in Rafael's book. The legends fascinated her, especially one about a tribe of giant gods who could make the earth tremble, and a regional mermaid myth concerning pink river dolphins, distant relatives of the Amazonian Indians, who stole women away from the tribe and impregnated them. Although she had no desire to pass judgment, she couldn't help thinking that some women could find this a rather handy excuse.

The clouds grew darker, lower, more threatening by the minute. Although she realized that she trusted Alec implicitly to get her back to camp safely, K.J. was relieved when they were back on the broader river, where they'd have a much better chance of riding out any storm.

"These myths are fascinating," she said, when she sensed Alec beginning to relax. Although she knew he was still disappointed, the tenseness that had hung over them like the moist jungle air had lessened.

"Rafael thought it important to get them down in writing, before the elders all died off, taking the stories with them," Alec revealed.

"I'm glad. So many people don't think to do that in time."

She wished she knew more about her own roots, her own family stories. But her parents had died before they'd passed on all that many stories, and her grandmother's accounts had always been more morality tale than Campbell family lore, carefully chosen to convince her young charge to toe the straight and narrow.

"They've got me looking forward to the festival."

"Don't expect it to be all that authentic," he warned.

"Why not?"

"Because it's mostly an extravaganza Rafael made up."

"Why would he do that?"

"Because the actual ceremonies didn't prove to be what people wanted. They weren't flashy enough. If tourists are going to come all the way here, they want their fantasies confirmed. They want something out of *Tarzan and the Jewels of Opar.* They want savages and sacrifice and lots of sex."

"Oh." Once again they were back to that sex thing. "That's sad."

Alec shrugged. "Not really. The fake ceremony makes a lot of money, the members of the tribe all know it's a performance, and in a way, it keeps the true rites pure because the locals don't have to risk contaminating their magic by doing it in front of outsiders."

K.J. thought about that and decided, not for the first time, that this was definitely the strangest, most com-

plex place she'd ever been. And considering some of
the locations she'd visited with her parents those first
nine years of her life, that was really saying something.

# 12

THE RAIN CAME as Alec had predicted, early and hard.
At first Kate wanted to do as he instructed—stay belowdecks out of the weather. But though she trusted
his ability to steer the boat through any trouble, she
found being unable to see anything too unnerving.
Having already found a rubberized poncho in a trunk,
she put it on, and holding onto the railing, climbed
back on deck.

"What the hell do you think you're doing?" Alec
yelled over the roar of the wind and thunder.

He was wearing an identical poncho. As the boat
rocked viciously from side to side, Kate didn't want to
think about the fact that their schoolbus yellow color
was undoubtedly not a fashion statement, but a way
to make it easier to find them—or, more likely, their
bodies—if they were washed into the roiling water.

"It's such a lovely day, I thought I'd take a little
stroll around the deck."

His eyes narrowed. Then his lips quirked and he
shook his head. "Absolutely crazy," he muttered. "At
least stay beneath the awning. I don't suppose you
happen to know how to tie a bowline knot?"

"Actually, I do. My grandmother summered in
Newport. Naturally, I learned how to sail." The words
were no sooner out of her mouth than she realized
how snobby that might sound.

But if he was offended, Alec didn't show it. "Good. Then tie that rope around your waist."

"Aye, Captain." She snapped a brisk salute that only earned another shake of his head before he turned all his attention back to the river.

Earlier, the Amazon had been smooth—not glassy, since it carried too much mud and silt for that—but smooth as a mug of hot chocolate. Now it was a racing tide of boiling white water, swirling mist that rose over them like smoke. More than once they dropped into a trough, causing a good two-thirds of the boat to sink beneath the waterline.

Just when K.J. was certain that they were going to capsize, Alec would steer them out of the swirling vortex and they'd bob back to the surface like a cork.

There were times when it seemed as if the entire river was pouring down on them. Enormous uprooted trees rushed toward the boat, half-hidden in the current, but somehow Alec managed to dodge them like bullets. Or, she thought, an enemy's arrows. Once again she had absolutely no trouble seeing him on a wide green battlefield, waging war to the wail of bagpipes.

He was amazingly skillful, but it took more than skill to keep them from sweeping into the maelstrom. More than courage. It took an amazing amount of patience. More than she would have thought any one man could possess.

She tried not to shudder at the sight of an anaconda draped around a tree, and failed. Okay, she decided, it took one heck of a lot courage, too. Which Alec appeared to have in spades.

Then, as if someone had turned off a shower faucet, the pelting rain stopped as abruptly as it had begun. A moment later, the boat surged beyond the rapids, dropping back into the wide, surprisingly calm, lazy red-brown river.

"I've never experienced anything like that in my life before!"

Sometime during the wild ride, the wind had whipped the canvas awning from two of the corner fasteners, providing scant protection against the rain that had been falling on them like water being poured from a boot. The hood of the poncho had fallen back onto her shoulders, allowing her head to get drenched. But K.J. wasn't worried about that. Not when she felt so intensely alive.

"It was even better than the Matterhorn and Mr. Toad's Wild Ride put together." Her sixth-grade class had taken a spring break trip to Disney World, and although her grandmother had nearly refused to let her go, fortunately, her teacher's arguments had prevailed.

"Who would have guessed it?" With things now safely under control, Alec came back to untie the rope that had kept her safely on deck. "Katherine Jeanne Campbell Mackenzie, adrenaline junky." He smiled at her unbridled enthusiasm.

K.J. smiled back. Then managed, just barely, to stop herself from throwing her arms around his neck.

"I guess I'll have to take up hang gliding. Or rock climbing."

"Sounds like a plan," he agreed. "Since you've already done the white-water rafting."

"You were absolutely terrific, Alec."

Her hair was a wild, wet tangle that framed her face like drooping seaweed. Although yesterday's lobster red sunburn had cooled down to a lighter pink color, her nose had begun to peel. If she'd put lipstick on this morning, she'd chewed it off, leaving her lips unpainted and delectably kissable. But gazing down at the lingering excitement and pleasure in her eyes, Alec decided that he'd never seen her look more lovely.

Because the adrenaline was still pumping through his own veins and because he could no longer be this close without touching her, he cupped her cheek in his palm and skimmed the pad of his thumb against the corner of her smiling lips.

"You were pretty terrific yourself. Most women—hell, most people—would have been screaming their heads off."

"I think I did," she admitted.

"Only when we took that one deep nosedive. But I didn't really hear you over my own shouting."

They shared a laugh over the near-death experience that was now safely behind them. Then K.J.'s eyes turned solemn. "I trusted you."

He closed his eyes briefly, savoring those three words. They weren't quite the ones he'd wanted to hear, but they were close enough. For now.

"I'd better get back to work."

When her answer stuck in her emotion-clogged throat, K.J. merely nodded.

He touched her again, just a hand to her wet hair, which she was certain must look like a rusty Brillo pad. Then he turned away to resume steering the boat back to the village.

K.J. retrieved her book from her waistband, where she'd stuffed it in an attempt to keep it dry. Fortunately, for the most part she'd succeeded, although a few of the pages were a bit water swollen.

She knew the book would forever be a souvenir—and a reminder—of this amazing day. Not that she'd need a physical reminder. The memory of Alec steering the small boat safely through those treacherous rapids would stay with her forever.

She tried to read, but was still jazzed enough that she couldn't concentrate. So she stood back up and leaned against the railing, watching the lush green jungle slip by.

"Are those what I think they are?" she asked, pointing at the brown things floating in the water near the bank. Things that appeared a bit too pebbly for logs.

He nodded. "Caiman."

"Terrific." She backed a step away.

"You don't have to worry—they're not like piranhas or anacondas," he assured her. "According to the locals, they only take small pieces out of you."

"Well, that's reassuring," she said dryly.

His grin was quick and devilish. "Unfortunately, they're usually the wrong pieces."

She tried not to smile, and failed.

K.J. was surprised at how comfortable she felt with Alec during the rest of the trip home. Then later, when they returned to the village and he stayed in the hut to pore over his charts and maps while she took advantage of the shower, she felt just as at ease.

He was working at the computer when she succumbed to the lure of the hammock and settled down for another nap. He was still there when she awoke an hour later.

"I can't believe this." She sat up and rubbed her eyes. "I've never been this lazy."

"You're not lazy. It just takes awhile to get acclimated to the heat and humidity."

"I suppose so. How long did it take you?"

"A week. Ten days."

"That long," she murmured.

"Yeah."

Another of those now-familiar silences settled over them. What they both left unstated was the fact that she wouldn't be staying here in Santa Clara long enough to get acclimatized.

"Well," he said, pushing up from the makeshift desk, "it's not that long until the festival starts. I guess I should leave you alone to change into your party dress."

"What makes you think I even brought a dress?"

"Didn't you?"

"Well, yes," she admitted reluctantly. "But only because my tour book suggested that it might be cooler." No way was she going to admit that she'd bought it just in case she needed a little extra ammunition to convince Alec to see things her way.

"It just might be." He reached into a drawer of the bamboo chest and took out another small handcrafted jar. "Just be certain to rub this on before you get dressed," he said. "It'll help keep the mosquitoes away."

"I brought repellent."

"This works better."

She opened the jar and scooped a bit of the pale green cream onto her finger, then brought it up to her nose. "It also smells a lot better."

"That, too."

Their eyes met once again, and in that suspended moment K.J. saw both desire and regret in Alec's gaze. She had no trouble recognizing the emotions, since she was feeling them herself.

"Well," he said again, "I'd better get going. Why don't I pick you up about six-thirty?"

"That sounds fine." Something suddenly occurred to her. "This will be our first date."

Instead of laughing at the ridiculousness of the situation—two married people about to get a divorce having a first date thousands of miles away from home—Alec seemed to be thinking that over.

"Better late than never," he decided.

He touched her again, just the slow swipe of his knuckles up her cheek as he passed the hammock, then left the hut. It wasn't until he'd gone that K.J. belatedly realized that her scold had been strangely silent all day.

Not wanting to push her luck—no point in waking sleeping dragons, she decided—she immediately put that thought out of her mind.

ALEC COULDN'T BELIEVE IT. As he stood outside the door of the hut two hours later—his hut, he reminded himself—he felt ridiculously like a pimply faced kid on his way to his first prom. With the head cheerleader, no less.

Biting back his anxiety, he rubbed his jaw, which he'd shaved for the second time today—definitely a record since his arrival in the jungle. Then he took a deep breath that he hoped would calm him but didn't, and knocked on the door.

The door opened instantly, making him wonder if perhaps she'd been just as anxious waiting for him. Then he took in the sight of her and that question—along with any possibility of coherent thought—fled his mind.

He wondered if Kate had any idea what a vision she made, with her fiery hair in that artful tousle atop her head, a style that suggested a single tug of a pin would send it cascading over her shoulders. He thought he detected the faintest touch of makeup, but she'd applied it with such a light hand he couldn't tell if the soft color in her cheeks and the light in her emerald eyes was due to cosmetics or emotion.

There was nothing overtly sexy about the simple off-the-shoulder dress. Once again he couldn't help noticing that she'd lost a great deal of weight, weight she couldn't really afford to lose. Yet the cream cotton brightened with a tropical flower print skimmed her body in a way that hinted at pleasures beneath. As he made an appreciative masculine perusal, Alec realized that he'd never before realized exactly how sexy a woman's calf could be.

"If you're trying to get me to change my mind about the divorce, you're definitely going about it the right way, sweetheart."

The color in her cheeks deepened. "That's not what I'm trying to do."

"Too bad." He took the flower he'd picked on the way from Rafael's hut and slipped it into her hair. "It's not exactly the requisite wrist corsage, but it reminded me of you."

The bloom was the color of newly churned cream with deepening pink interior petals. As he lifted it to her hair, K.J. had caught a glimpse of the dew drop at the heart of the deep rose center.

"It's lovely. And that was very thoughtful of you." She lifted a hand to her hair. "And why would I want a corsage?"

He shrugged, feeling foolish. "This feels a bit like a prom date. Which would call for a proper corsage in a nice little box with the florist's name on it."

"I never went to a prom, but I think I'd rather have this."

"I'm glad. And how could you not have gone to a prom?"

"I went to an all-girls school."

"Still, you had to have gone to some dances with boys from nearby schools." He'd gone to a military academy, but had garnered more than his share of invitations from local girls.

"Actually, I never did."

"Were all the boys in New England blind?"

"Not really. They wanted curvaceous blondes. I was too tall, too skinny, and my hair was definitely too red."

"Obviously blind and stupid to boot," Alec decided. His gray eyes took another slow, appreciative perusal. "You really are the most incredible creature."

"Thank you."

Oh, God, whenever he looked at her that way, K.J. couldn't help wondering if she was really doing the right thing, asking for the divorce. Then she remembered how quickly he'd given in and decided that perhaps the attraction they were both obviously feeling really wasn't the forever-after kind.

But it sure wasn't bad for what it was.

She skimmed an appreciative glance over him. "You look pretty good yourself." Better than good. He looked gorgeous in a faded blue chambray work shirt and another pair of worn-white-at-the-seams jeans that hugged his sex in a way her fingers were aching to.

He toyed with the dangling pink seashell earrings some feminine impulse had had her purchase when she'd bought the native straw hat. "You know, if you're still uncomfortable attending the fertility ritual, we could always just stay home. Watch a little TV, send out for a pizza, neck in the hammock—"

"We don't have a television. And it's a very long way for Dominos to deliver."

"True." His grin belied his sigh. "I suppose that just

leaves us with the necking part of the evening." His fingers brushed the pastel shells aside; his teeth nipped delicately at her earlobe.

"Alec." It was more shimmering sigh than complaint.

"Is that a yes?" His clever hand traced the outline of a hibiscus just below her right breast. When his sly, wicked fingers brushed against her nipple, K.J.'s heart began to thunder in her chest.

"You promised." Even as she tried to protest, she tilted her head back, inviting the touch of his lips.

Alec instantly obliged. "True." Her skin there was as pale and silky as the blossom in her hair. His tongue dipped into the hollow at the base of her throat and tasted warmth. And desire. "I also promised not to do anything you truly don't want me to do."

She was swaying, as if they were back on the rolling deck of his boat. She lifted her strangely heavy hands to his shoulders for balance. "I don't want this."

"Liar." He leaned back just enough to look down into her unfocused eyes. "I don't suppose you'd be willing to kiss me and tell me that."

"Ah, another test." She smiled up at him as her vision cleared. "I've always been very good at tests."

He smiled back, enjoying this flirtatious moment. Enjoying her. "So have I. Which should make this even more interesting."

His mouth was warm as it claimed hers, his body hard against her softly yielding one, his arms so strong, so right, as they encircled her and drew her even closer. How was it, she wondered when she heard his husky moan of pleasure mingled with a deep male need, that this man could make her feel both soft and strong all at the same time?

Practically purring herself, she lifted her arms and

slid her fingers through his hair—thick, shaggy silk. "We can't do this."

"I'd say we're doing it pretty damn well." Without taking his mouth from hers, he lifted her off her feet, holding her tight against him.

"It's a mistake." With her legs wrapped around him, she began scattering a blizzard of kisses over his throat, his face—that rugged, gorgeous face.

"That's your opinion." The way she had him in a vice grip between those long coltish legs made him feel about to explode. "Personally, I think it's long overdue."

She heard a thundering of bass percussion and realized it wasn't her heart, but the pounding of tribal drums. "The festival…"

"Screw the festival." His hands were beneath her skirt, his fingers digging into the silky skin bared by the high cut of her cotton panties. "It's not real, anyway."

She gasped at his intimate touch, at the way he was grinding against her.

"Stay here, Kate." Alec realized he was on the verge of begging. Worse yet, he didn't care. "Stay with me." He braced his feet. Then, lifting her still higher, he put his mouth on her breast, dampening the cotton. "Stay here where you belong."

Oh, how she wanted to! As much as she'd ever wanted anything in her life. Her need for him was every bit as strong as her need to breathe. She'd never felt so defenseless.

"I can't." She dragged in a painful breath. "You promised, Alec. We're getting a divorce and you're coming to New York with me."

"Come with me instead." He moved to her other breast, doing things with his mouth and teeth that had her trembling like a willow in a hurricane. "I'll take you places you've never been, Kate. Wonderful, magical places."

Of that she had not a single doubt. She also still believed, deep down inside, that sex—even the hottest, most thrilling of her life—wasn't anything to base a long-term commitment on.

"Oh, Alec." She dragged her mouth away from his. "Don't you see? I want you, too. So much I can't bear it. But it's not enough."

He went as still as stone, then slowly lowered her back to the ground. As she stood there, still held tight against his rock-hard body, Kate could feel him garnering control, nerve by nerve, muscle by muscle.

He would, Alec assured himself as he gathered up the scattered threads of his patience, maintain his control if it killed him. "Your call."

His voice was distant, but roughened with a hunger K.J. was feeling herself.

She placed a conciliatory hand on his arm and felt the muscle turn to a boulder beneath her fingertips. "I'm sorry."

Alec couldn't decide whether to curse her or himself. In the end he did neither. "You don't have to apologize, Katherine Jeanne. It's a woman's prerogative to change her mind."

"It's also a woman's responsibility not to promise things she's not willing to carry out."

As he looked down into her miserable face, Alec felt his irritation fading away. Sympathy stirred. "Are you always this tough on yourself?"

"There are rules." She briefly closed her eyes at the tender touch of his fingers skimming up her cheekbone. "Sensible people follow them."

He wondered if that was his Kate talking, or her

pessimistic little voice. "And lose out on a helluva lot of fun in the meantime." Because it was easier to laugh than to cry, he shook his head and managed a crooked smile. "Now, before I put us to another test, we'd better get going."

Kate opened her mouth to thank him, but something hard and flinty in his eyes stopped her. She merely nodded instead and smoothed the rumpled cotton beneath her hands.

Alec watched those lily-white hands move from her chest to her hips, and felt a now-familiar surge of need.

As they left the hut, he couldn't decide which of them was crazier. Then decided it probably didn't matter, since they were both undoubtedly flat-out nuts.

# 13

AS THEY WALKED across the village square, the equatorial sun was melting into a glorious El Greco landscape of shimmering blues and blinding oranges. A young boy, no more than six or seven, ran in front of them, a brilliant cockatoo perched on his shoulder.

"If I'd given it any thought, I would have imagined the jungle being totally green," K.J. murmured. "But the color is almost blinding. I feel like Dorothy, when she landed in Oz and suddenly everything went from black-and-white to Technicolor."

"It is dazzling," Alec agreed. "And, as stubborn as it is about giving up its secrets, a part of it gets into your blood."

"That sounds suspiciously as if you're considering staying."

"Nah. I'll probably come back, if for no other reason than to check in and see how Rafael's doing and play uncle to his kids, when he finally settles down and has some. But once I find the barge, I've got a book to write. And a Viking ship loaded with plundered Celtic artifacts to recover off the coast of Lapland."

Once again, K.J. thought how much like her father Alec was. George Campbell would not only have liked her husband, he would have respected him as well. He also, she suspected, would not have been happy about her choice to travel a safer, more secure path in life.

However, she thought with a quick flash of Campbell temper, if her father had wanted her to be more daring, then he should have managed to stay alive long enough to act as a role model, rather than sending her into the clutches of the grim and always proper mother he'd been estranged from for years before K.J. was even born.

"Penny for your thoughts," Alec murmured.

"I was just thinking about my father and how excited he would have been about tonight." She only hoped she could do her legacy justice.

"I wish I could have met him."

"He would have liked you."

"Even after I took his baby girl away?"

K.J. returned his smile. "All you'd have to do is praise his work and he'd be putty in your hands." As she was.

"That would be easy enough." Since the sun had set, she'd left her hat back at the hut, allowing him to drop a quick friendly kiss atop her head. "Even easier would be praising him on his lovely daughter."

Fortunately, their arrival at the lodge, where Rafael was waiting to greet them, precluded K.J. from having to answer that flattering statement.

The huge communal ceremonial lodge, Alec told K.J., had, like the sleeping lodge, been built with government grants Rafael had acquired. The men sat cross-legged on reed mats on one side of the oval room, the women and children on another. They were all adorned with body paint, which Alec explained was believed to invoke friendly spirits.

At the far end of the large space was a group of young, half-naked adolescent girls whose hair had been cut short, which, Alec told her, signaled their arrival at the threshold of womanhood.

"That coming of age ceremony is one of the most important of the tribal cycle," he murmured as they took their place among the group of Europeans and Americans who'd been given positions of honor on the east—and thus more holy—side of the lodge. "Even more important than the marriage rite."

"Which means it isn't for public display?"

"Exactly."

K.J. nodded her approval. "I'm glad. That's a very personal time for a girl. I'd feel as if I were intruding."

Alec was pleased by her instant understanding and wondered how much of her ability to so quickly accept other cultures came from spending her first nine years with her gypsy parents.

Apparently believing that a well-fed audience was a receptive audience, the tribe had prepared a feast for their visitors.

Still having secretly feared being served termite appetizers, K.J. was relieved when the food was not only vaguely familiar, but delicious. The feast began with slices of smoked fish surrounded by sweet black grapes that were nearly the size of golf balls. While K.J. had been exploring the river with Alec, the women had wrapped bananas and manioc cakes in wild banana leaves and cooked them among fire-heated stones.

A tapir—or wild pig—had been roasted to a turn in a pit and went perfectly with the stone-cooked sweet potatoes. K.J. also found the mutum, which was the size of a wild turkey and served with a side of boiled rice, delicious. She did, however, politely pass on the armadillo that had been cooked in its shell.

"This punch is absolutely delicious," K.J. said as she smilingly accepted another gourdful of bright orange fruit punch from a loincloth-clad waiter wearing a necklace of bright macaw feathers. She took an appreciative sip. "What's it made of, anyway?" It tasted vaguely familiar, but she couldn't quite pinpoint it.

"It's from the pupunha palm—or peach palm. With some coconut milk mixed in."

"That explains it." She nodded. "It's like a piña colada. With peaches instead of pineapple. I'm going to have to get the recipe."

Alec wondered how she'd feel if she knew the fruit was prepared by first being masticated by the old, toothless women of the tribe, who'd then spit the mash into a dugout canoe, where it was covered with palm leaves and allowed to ferment in the heat.

"I'd be a little careful," he warned. "It packs quite a punch."

"I'm fine." She smiled up at him. "Better than fine." She leaned back on her elbows beside him. "I can't remember when I've felt so relaxed."

"That probably has something to do with the fact that that's your third gourd of pupunha."

"That's not it at all." Her smile widened and she aimed a kiss at his cheek that missed and hit his jaw. "It's getting away from the city."

She sighed happily as she watched a man toss something onto the fire, which had burned down to embers. An incense-scented cloud rose from the hot rocks, then drifted over the room like wisps of fog.

When the man sat down again, a group of children rose and began to march around the oval circle of onlookers. They were, she realized, the tribal orchestra. Three boys were playing amazingly well on reed flutes, while four others were blowing into hard palms, creating an oboelike sound. A pair of boys on the brink of adolescence pounded barehanded on hollow drums, setting the pace for the dancers, who'd entered the lodge.

Young women dressed in skirts of shredded tree bark and wristlets and anklets of bright feathers moved to the pulsing rhythm, their feet shuffling on the packed dirt floor, their hips swaying in a hulalike motion. Accustomed to the Western female fanaticism concerning a perfect Barbie doll body, K.J. was envious at the way they seemed so unconcerned about their near nakedness. Some tummies were perhaps more rounded than the Western ideal, some breasts not as pert. But from their sensual movements and the bright light of feminine confidence in their flashing dark eyes, K.J. suspected none of them suffered any body-image insecurity.

And why should they? she mused, remembering what Alec had told her about this being a matriarchal society. Since they possessed the power, they could also create the ideal of feminine beauty in their own individual image.

That thought had her wondering if in this culture, perhaps it was the men who had to worry about staying fit and virile. If so, she decided, skimming a surreptitious sideways glance at the man lounging beside her, Alec would undoubtedly be considered the most desirable male in the village. Which her little encounter with Sonia yesterday had already suggested.

And speaking of Sonia…K.J. was not at all pleased by the way she'd positioned herself near them, looking for all the world like some sort of lush female fertility statue come to life.

An older man, painted in maroon dye, joined the women at the center of the circle and began to chant. He was wearing leglets of hollow nuts that rattled as he shuffled his feet. What Alec told K.J. were armadillo claws around his wrists and shiny yellow jaguar teeth around his neck reminded K.J. uncomfortably of her middle-of-the-night encounter. The man was wearing a second necklace—a single, highly polished pink quartz pendant strung on twine.

"That's considered a source of power," Alec explained, "since he found it while wandering lost during his dream-journey—the spiritual, hallucinogenic trip all would-be medicine men have to survive before being allowed to practice their spiritual arts."

The pace of the music quickened. The medicine man's chanting grew louder. In his left hand he began whirling a reed stick that, when hit with his right hand, created a high singing sound that vibrated through the smoky lodge. The women's dance had become a blatant invitation as they swayed seductively in front of the men, eyes flashing sensual messages that backed up the erotic motion of their hips.

Each time a man jumped up, eager to dance with a woman, he faced a possible rebuff. Those who were allowed to join in the dance were celebrated with a roar of approval from the crowd.

It was soon apparent that the visitors were not going to be left on the sidelines as mere observers. While the young women danced, older ones worked the perimeter of the crowd, urging the *civilizadas* to their feet. One girl, in her early twenties, with a waist-length fall of platinum blond hair, was the first to succumb, tossing off her T-shirt and bra with abandonment. As she laughed and teased the man who was obviously her boyfriend, the crowd applauded both her daring and her skill.

Other women followed. And although a very strong part of K.J. yearned to join them, her little voice had returned to keep her in her place.

*It's a disgraceful display of things that should be kept private between a man and a woman,* it said in that voice that was so eerily like her grandmother's. For not the first time K.J. was forced to wonder how on earth Helen Campbell had ever loosened up enough to engage in the sex necessary to have a son.

But K.J. didn't think it was all that disgraceful. On the contrary, she mused, as she sipped on another gourd of the tasty punch, the erotic, hedonistic dance was the closest thing to how she felt whenever Alec touched her. Kissed her. Even looked at her with those wicked silver eyes. Which was why, when a trio of laughing women ganged up on her, pulling her to her feet and encouraging her to lose herself in the moment, she didn't even try to argue.

The unrelenting beat of the drums echoed all the way to the marrow of her bones; the sexy wail of the handcrafted reed instruments set her blood thrumming in her veins. And the way Alec was looking at her—only at her—made her body glow with an inner heat that had nothing to do with the smoldering coals and hot rocks.

She was no longer Katherine Jeanne Campbell, the girl who always got straight A's and had won the state champion debating medal. She was no longer the nervous, swept-away-by-romance bride who'd married a man who could have stepped from the pages of the books she edited.

She was Woman. An all-powerful female who felt not the slightest need to hide her sexuality beneath drab suits and tidy hairdos. She was a woman who knew what she wanted and had no qualms about going after her perfect mate. After Alec.

As she stood in front of him, her eyes locked on his, Alec belatedly realized he'd made a tactical battlefield error. He'd brought Kate here tonight to loosen her up. In that, at least, he'd been successful.

Better than successful, he thought as she slipped the flowered cotton dress off one shoulder with a flirtatious flair that could have put Gypsy Rose Lee to shame. If she was any looser, she wouldn't be able to stand up. Or to keep moving her slender hips in a way that made him want to grab hold and go along for the wild ride. He'd planned to seduce his wife tonight; what he hadn't counted on was her seducing him.

She languidly lifted her arms to comb her fingers through the wild spirals of fiery curls in a way that thrust her breasts invitingly toward him, allowing him to observe the way the nipples were pressing against the thin material. Alec felt his heart pounding in his head, his ears. His loins.

Recklessness blazed in her eyes, radiated from the bump and grind of her hips. Alec never would have guessed that she'd even known how to move that way.

"Good God, Kate." It was half curse, half groan.

"What's the matter, Alec?" She leaned toward him, her breasts at eye level as she cupped his face between her silky smooth palms. "Does it disturb your male ego to surrender control?" She touched her tongue against the tip of her index finger, then skimmed it along the seam of his lips. The fingertip was wet, his skin was hot; Alec imagined he could hear the resulting hiss of steam.

"Actually..." He swallowed past the knot of lust when the word came out sounding half-choked. "Actually, I'm enjoying the show."

"I'm glad." Her smile was nothing less than beatific. It was also dangerous. Alec figured that Salome must have looked a lot like Kate while she'd been discarding all those veils. Right before she'd demanded the Baptist's head on a platter. Kate touched her mouth against Alec's, allowed a brief tangle of tongues, then backed away again like the seductress she'd amazingly metamorphosed into. "I want you to enjoy yourself tonight, Alec."

She began to move again, her hands caressing their way down her sides, over the slight flare of hips and across her thighs in a way that had him almost swallowing his tongue. "I intend for both of us to enjoy ourselves."

Her eyes holding his with the sheer strength of her feminine will, she slipped the dress off the other shoulder. It was now clinging to the crests of her breasts in a way that had a hot, virile hunger pumping through his blood. He wanted to rip her dress off her, cup her breasts in his hands, take them into his mouth and suck hard enough to make her cry out.

She shimmied in a remarkable way that had the dress falling down to her waist, revealing breasts barely covered by a wisp of ivory lace nearly the same color as her creamy flesh.

Although he'd never thought of himself as a cowardly man, Alec had never been more afraid than he was at this minute. Afraid of her. Of the immensity of the emotions she could make him feel.

"This time I'm the one doing the choosing." She crooked a finger at him; her eyes, dark and smoky and, he thought, just a bit glazed, beckoned. "And I choose you."

Alec didn't wait for a second invitation. He was on his feet with her in his arms in an instant. "It's about time."

"I know." She twined her arms around his neck and practically melded into him. "It feels so good, doesn't it?'' Her silken lips nuzzled at his throat. "You and me together like this."

"Damn good." He skimmed his hands up her back, then down again, slowly, enjoying the way he could make her tremble, enjoying the way she warmed beneath his caressing touch. As his blood beat in time to the pulsating drumbeat, he cupped her hips and lifted her against him. "But it could be a lot better."

"Yes." She tilted her head back and smiled up at him. "I think we've danced enough," she decided. "I also believe it's time we moved this to a more private location."

Her words were slurred, her eyes perhaps just a bit brighter than they should have been. When he twirled her in a way that didn't suit the jungle beat, he felt her stumble.

"I hate like hell to bring this up," he said, reluctantly pulling the dress back up. "But I think, sweetheart, that you're smashed."

"I am not." She twined her arms tighter around him and pressed her mouth to his. "I'm just a little bit tipsy, that's all." Her lips plucked at his, punctuating her faintly slurred words. "I know exactly what I'm doing."

The muscles in his stomach tightened, then twisted like wrought iron. "That's what you think now." He reminded himself that the Mackenzies had always been men of honor. And men of honor did not take advantage of drunk, vulnerable women. "But you're not thinking straight, Katherine Jeanne."

His use of her formal name had her tilting her head back to gaze up at him again. "You look so serious."

Because he was horribly tempted to capture that pouting mouth, to plunder that slender body, Alec put her a bit away from him. "This is serious."

"I know." She sighed. "It always seems to be with us, doesn't it? Any reasonable people would have just allowed themselves a hot, one-night fling, then moved on in the morning."

"That's pretty much what we did," he stated.

"True." She closed the scant distance between them and rested her cheek against his shoulder. "But we complicated things by getting married." She sighed again. "Why can't it ever be simple between us, Alec?"

Tenderness warred with lust. Love with passion. Alec pressed his lips against her temple. "Because if it were simple, it would just be sex." He tipped her face back up to his with a mere touch of a finger beneath her chin. "And you'd never settle for that."

She was having a little bit of trouble focusing, but assured herself it was merely her eyes watering from the incense. "Would you?" she asked, honestly wanting—needing—to know. "Would you settle for just sex?"

It was not the time or place to be having this discussion. But, Alec reminded himself, it was probably long overdue. "I have." He watched the disappointment cloud her eyes and wondered if she even understood that a divorce was the last thing she wanted. "In the past." With his thumb, he soothed the line that was etching itself between her tawny brows. "But not with you, Kate." Alec lowered his head until his lips were a whisper away from hers. "Never with you."

"Oh, God." The words shuddered out as she trembled. "I want you, Alec. So much." Her eyes were swimming now. She blinked furiously at the hot moisture. "Too much."

"I want you, too." He resisted the lure of her lips, knowing that to kiss her here, now, would be madness, since he wouldn't be able to stop. "And I need you, Kate. More than I need to draw my next breath."

"Then for God's sake, take me." Her moist eyes were eloquent with emotion. "Now. Before either of us comes to our senses."

"I will." He linked their fingers together and lifted their joined hands to his lips. His eyes lanced into hers. "But not for God's sake, Kate. And not just for yours. Or mine." His heart was pounding in his throat like the beat of the tribal drums, making words difficult. "But ours."

He watched the smooth muscles in her throat as she swallowed, then nodded. "Ours." It was only a whisper, impossible to hear over the din now filling the smoky lodge. But Alec didn't miss reading the single word of commitment on her lips. Or the uncensored love in her incredible blue eyes.

He wanted to carry her out of the room like some conquering soldier. No, he thought as he felt his heart tumble, then soften, as it always seemed to do whenever he was around her. He wanted to carry her like he had that first night when, over her breathless, laughing protests, he'd played bridegroom by carrying her over the threshold.

"How's your imagination?" he asked.

"Right now?" she answered. "Incredibly vivid."

"Good." Deciding that she couldn't have carried on that serious conversation if she were too looped on the pupunha, he scooped her into his arms. "It was okay to be Kate and Bogie while we were on the river. But tonight I'm switching movies. And roles." Because he couldn't resist, he touched his lips to hers in a kiss that, while brief, still managed to rock him to his toes. "Try thinking of me as Gable."

"I don't need to." Her lips lifted to his and clung. "I

don't want Bogie, Alec. And I don't need Gable carrying me up some sweeping antebellum staircase."
Mindless of their audience as they made their way through the throng of dancers to the door, she kissed his jaw. "All I need—all I want—is you."

It was the admission he'd been waiting for. The muscles in his stomach relaxed even as his heart spiked with anticipation.

"Believe me, sweetheart," he said with a rough laugh, "I know the feeling."

## 14

K.J. FELT AS IF SHE WERE floating as Alec carried her across the village square, heading out into the forest. The monsoon clouds had blown away, leaving patches of star-studded sky that glittered like spilled diamonds on a tray of ebony velvet.

Fireflies—thousands of them—flitted around them, lighting the way like dancing stars. Flaming torches burning outside the ceremonial area gave the sky surrounding them a faintly orange glow.

Fortunately, the night sounds that had kept sleep at bay last night were silent. Or perhaps, she thought, she simply couldn't hear them over the sound of her blood pounding in her ears.

As soon as they entered the hut, before he even put her down, Alec lit the lantern. The inky darkness suddenly glowed as if brightened by the equatorial sun.

"We don't need a light," she murmured, suddenly unwilling to let him see exactly how much weight she'd lost during their time apart.

"I do." He put her gently onto her feet beside the hammock, holding on to her shoulders when she swayed ever so slightly. "I want to watch you while I undress you, Kate." He skimmed a kiss up her cheek. "I want to touch and taste and see every silken inch of you."

The sparklerlike touch of his lips moved back down to her jaw. "I intend to see the heat in your remarkable blue eyes when I take you into the flames." His tongue traced down her throat. "And I'm looking forward to seeing the warm, satisfied pleasure in them when we end up safe in each other's arms on the other side."

She was swaying again, not from the drink, but from the intoxicating feel of his lips at her collarbone, the tug of his teeth on her earlobe.

After all this time apart, months during which he claimed to have been celibate, K.J. would have expected him to take her quickly the first time. She'd prepared herself to be swept instantly into the heat. But to her surprise, he seemed in no hurry to undress her. Instead, for a long, immeasurable time, he made love to her with only his mouth. And with seductive words designed to make her burn.

"Have I ever told you that I love your chin?" he murmured as he captured it between his teeth.

"I believe I would have remembered you mentioning that."

"I do." His tongue soothed the skin that had turned from yesterday's lobster red to seashell pink. "It reminds me of a fox. A stubborn Scots fox," he amended as he nibbled kisses along her jawline. "There are times when you stick it out in that unspoken challenge that would drive the most patient of men to distraction.... But right beneath it there's this lovely expanse of creamy silk." The trail of knee-weakening kisses moved slowly, inexorably down her throat. "The kind that creates an entirely different type of distraction."

"Alec." K.J. clung to his shoulders. "Please." Her voice was as ragged as her nerves. "Make love to me."

"That's precisely what I'm doing." His fingers skimmed along her collarbone in a feathery caress. "But I've learned that down here in the jungle heat, it's best to pace myself." He kissed his way from throat to shoulder. Then back again. "To take my time." When he repeated the tender torment, creating a trail of heat along her other collarbone, a purr of pleasure sounded in her throat. "After all, we've all the time in the world."

That wasn't quite accurate. In fact, the sad truth was that it wasn't the least bit true. But unwilling to destroy this magic moment by injecting reality into it, Kate didn't argue. Especially now that he'd moved on to the undressing part of the evening.

Possessing an almost otherwordly patience she suspected was vital in the treasure-hunting business, he took his time with that as well, unbuttoning the first button, folding back the brightly flowered cotton and kissing the exposed bit of bared flesh before moving on to the second.

"You realize, of course," she protested with a shaky laugh as he finally moved on to the third button, "that you're driving me crazy."

"Ah, but I thought we'd already determined that you were crazy." Without taking his eyes from hers, he smiled, a slow, lazy smile of satisfaction as he slipped the button free. "And I mean that," he drawled, "in the very best way."

Even as she smiled back, K.J. realized how true those words were. She was absolutely, certifiably crazy. About this man who could make her want to laugh with pleasure and weep with frustration all at the same time.

Just when she was certain she'd die from impatience, he reached the button at her waist and slipped the dress off her shoulders. After treating the crest of her breasts to a torment just as prolonged, just as sweet, he tugged the dress down the rest of the way, where it pooled around her feet like a spilled bouquet of bright tropical blossoms.

"I have never been able to decide what your skin reminds me of," he murmured as he unfastened her bra with a quick deft touch that suggested this was a man who definitely knew his way around women's clothing. After tossing the scrap of silk and lace onto the nearby tabletop, he moved his wide rough hands down her body.

"Sometimes I think it's like porcelain." His fingers traced concentric circles on each breast, one at a time, from rib cage to the dusky pink nipples that pebbled at his touch. "But porcelain is too hard." He cupped her right breast in his hand and took it into his mouth in a way that caused a corresponding tug deep inside her. "And cold."

"Alec..." K.J. didn't know how much longer she could survive this achingly slow seduction.

"God, I love the way you say my name," he murmured against her yielding flesh as he turned his attention to her left breast. "In that throaty voice laced with passion." He closed his teeth lightly around the tingling nipple, drawing a gasp, not of fear, but of pleasure from her. "You've no idea how many times in the past months that voice has tormented my sleep. Along with memories of exactly how warm and perfect you felt in my arms...which brings me back to the subject of your skin," he said, revealing that he was thinking far more clearly than she was at this moment. "Sometimes I think it reminds me of pearls, especially the way it glistens in the moonlight. But pearls aren't fragrant. Or nearly as soft."

As she moaned, the same way she always did in those fantasies that left him hot and stiff as a pike, Alec dropped to his knees and tugged her bikini panties down her hips, over her thighs, then her calves, following the path of the white cotton with his mouth.

As she dragged her fingers through his hair, K.J. wondered how and when he'd taken control. Not that she hadn't surrendered it willingly, she thought, crying out, just a little, as his teeth scraped her thigh. And although some women might feel uncomfortably vulnerable, being stripped naked by a man who was still fully dressed, K.J. was finding the situation incredibly erotic.

"So," he said, tormenting her further by ignoring that hot wet place that was aching for his touch, "I've narrowed it down to two things. Camellia petals..." his fingers skimmed a sensual path through the copper-penny-bright curls between her quaking thighs "...or sweet, rich cream." With that declaration, he flicked his tongue over the distended pink nub and felt her shatter like crystal.

She cried out his name, just as he'd vowed she would, but Alec wasn't nearly finished. Not by a long shot. Utilizing his hungry mouth and fingers as weapons, he drove her up even higher, again and again, until her muffled screams filled the steamy air around them and her muscles went as lax as water. Then and only then did Alec give into her breathless pleas and lower her to the hammock.

"I can't believe it," she gasped as she reached out toward him, amazed that after all that, she'd still want more. Need more. "What you do to me." The bulge in the front of his jeans made her ache in places that were still convulsing from her mind-blinding orgasms. "How you make me feel."

"It's us." He unbuttoned his own shirt with far more speed than he had hers, then flung it aside with a great deal less care. When those long dark fingers she could still feel dancing over her burning flesh moved to the metal button at the waist of his jeans, K.J. somehow managed to muster up the strength to object.

"No," she managed to whisper in a husky, sexy voice that didn't sound anything like her usual controlled one.

"No?" His hands froze. His every muscle appeared to stiffen to stone. K.J. watched in admiration as he fought for control over mind and body, and won.

"No." She was laughing now, not at him, but with a rich womanly pleasure she'd known only once before in her life. "I love what you do to me." Strangely, her orgasms seemed to have cleared her head, blowing away the misty clouds created by the incense and spiked punch. It was a good thing, too, she thought as she managed to rise to her knees on the swaying hemp, because riding this hammock was almost as tricky as riding those rapids earlier that day. "It's my turn. To do it back to you."

"Ah." He nodded. And relaxed. Just enough to ease the knot of tension that had settled between his shoulders. "I like a lady who believes in taking turns. It shows she plays well with others."

A year ago, she'd fumbled when she'd tried to undress him. Tonight, emboldened with feminine power, her own fingers were nearly as deft as his had been, flicking open the button, then lowering the metal zipper, tooth by tooth, fully intending to torment Alec as he had her.

But when his sex burst free, hard and hot and virile, all her good intentions disintegrated. How could she have forgotten how powerful he was? How beautiful? As she curled her fingers around his rigid length, K.J. knew that she hadn't forgotten a single thing. Which was why, she finally admitted, at least to herself, that she'd agreed to come down here in the first place.

Her motive hadn't been pride. Or even a promotion. She'd been coerced into nothing. The simple truth was that she'd trekked all this way because she'd been dying to find out whether everything between them was as strong and inevitable as she remembered.

A part of her had been hoping that she'd exaggerated their night together. But now, as she caressed him more intimately than she had any other man, loving him as he'd loved her, with fluttering hands and avid mouth, she realized that in truth, she'd underestimated the force of the power between them. If anything, it was even stronger than it had been that night.

Once he'd made the decision to make love to her, Alec had intended to be the one in charge. He'd wanted to make her scream, and he had. And as satisfying as that had been, he now realized that somehow, when he wasn't looking, he'd surrendered all control.

"Kate..." His hands tangled in her hair as her lips and tongue treated him to a torment sweeter than anything he'd ever known. Even better than their wedding night when, although she'd been eagerly open to anything he might propose, she'd always allowed him to lead. "You realize that you're killing me, here."

Her soft chuckle vibrated against his groin, sending jolts of lightning through his bloodstream. "Don't worry, Alec." Her fingers cupped the sensitive flesh beneath his shaft even as her tongue swirled, gathering in the pearly moisture at the tip. "I promise to be gentle." She released him just long enough to pull him down on top of her. "Because I'm not nearly finished with you yet."

With a strength he never would have suspected she

possessed, she rolled over, taking him with her, so that she was now the one on top, straddling his thighs.

Her eyes drank in the sight of him, sprawled beneath her, confident enough in his own strength to surrender the power. At least for now.

"God, I love your body," she breathed, as she splayed her fingers over his dark, moist chest.

"It's all yours," he managed to gasp as she kissed her way across his stomach, sharp stinging little kisses that felt like hot darts.

"I know." This time her smile was not Salome's, but Eve's, her gleaming blue eyes offering Alec all the gifts of Paradise.

As she undressed him, his muscles quivered under her hands and his flesh grew hot and moist beneath her lips. She moved like quicksilver over his body, drawing rumbling moans that echoed like thunder from deep inside him.

His breath burned like fire in his throat, his lungs. His blood pounded in his veins, his loins. And just when he was certain she was going to drive him mad, she rose over him, her hair curling like flames over her ivory shoulders.

"I've dreamed of us like this." Her lips curved in a faint, womanly smile. "Hot, wicked, wonderful dreams." With agonizing slowness she lowered herself onto him, taking him in, inch by throbbing inch.

The feel of her, warm and wet around him, aroused Alec mercilessly. "Join the club, sweetheart." When she began to rock against him in a slow, seductive rhythm designed to torment them both, his hunger turned voracious. His need brutal.

She arched her back, offering him her breasts, which he took into his mouth, lashing the hot silken flesh with teeth and tongue. She was moving faster now, the muscles of her thighs clamping tighter around his hips as she rode him, racing toward the peak.

His vision blurred, shimmering bloodred at the edges. Caught in the clutches of an unmanageable greed, he dug his fingers into her waist and arched off the hammock, surging upward into her, plunging, hammering against her as he drove them both blindly over the precipice.

"Oh," she gasped as she collapsed on top of him, spent and slick with sweat. "That was definitely better than the dreams."

"Absolutely." He tangled his fist in her damp hair, lifting her head so their eyes met. "Anyone ever tell you, Mrs. Mackenzie, that you are definitely one hot piece of—"

"Never." Her mouth, as she touched it to his, was curved in a smile. But her gaze was solemn. "There was never a reason. Until you."

"Until us," he corrected, shifting so they were lying face-to-face, chest-to-chest, thigh-to-thigh. "Together."

Since she knew she'd never be able to deny it, K.J. didn't even try. Instead, she just wrapped her arms around him and nuzzled close, enjoying the sound of the rain—which had begun again sometime during their lovemaking—on the tin roof, the rise and fall of his hard chest beneath her cheek and the touch of his hand as it roamed idly, contentedly, up and down her bare back.

"Oh, my God," K.J. moaned the next morning as the hot Amazonian sun shot flaming arrows into her already burning eyes. "I think I'm going to die."

"I told you to go easy on that stuff," Alec reminded her. "It was just a hangover waiting to happen."

She lifted her head to glare up at him, then wished she hadn't as more arrows pierced her skull. "I never get hangovers," she muttered.

"Well then, consider this another first," he said in a cheerful tone that made her want to smack him. But he was safe, because she didn't think she'd ever be able to move again. "Here."

She opened one bleary eye and tried to focus on the earthenware cup he was holding out toward her. "What's that?"

"A native remedy guaranteed to have you feeling like a new woman in no time at all."

"I've tried that new-woman stuff with you twice now, Alec. And both times it's turned out miserably."

Knowing exactly how badly her head was pounding, he decided not to take affront at the insult. "That's not what you were saying when you woke up in the middle of the night and attacked me again."

"Me, attack you?" She reluctantly pushed herself into a sitting position. "I seem to recall it being the other way around."

"That was the third time. After you'd already had your wicked way with me."

Heat surged into her cheeks as she remembered exactly how wicked they'd been. "I don't remember you complaining."

"Hey, I'm no fool." He shoved the cup toward her again. "Here. This really will make you feel better."

She reluctantly accepted it, took one whiff and drew in a sharp breath as her stomach roiled. "What's in it?"

"A secret blend of herbs."

"It looks like mud."

"Tastes like it, too," he assured her with a grin that

had her stomach flipping for an entirely different reason. "But it works like magic."

She gave the contents one last suspicious look, then closed her eyes, lifted the cup to her lips and swallowed what was, without a doubt, the most vile thing she'd ever tasted.

"Promise me one thing," she groaned as she flopped back onto the hammock.

"Anything," he said without hesitation.

"If I die, you'll still go to New York and do the auction."

"You're not going to die. But I am curious why you'd want me to do that, since it's a little difficult to get a posthumous promotion."

"It's a matter of honor."

"Ah." Alec nodded. Honor was something he both understood and approved of. "You've got yourself a deal." He bent down, brushed her hair off her forehead and dropped a light kiss on her clammy skin. "I'm going to go take a shower. Then I'll come back and we'll have a little breakfast—"

She flung her arm over her closed eyes and shuddered. "I really will die if I put anything in my stomach after that Amazonian mud."

"Actually, food is exactly what you need." He skimmed his knuckles in a slow sweep down the side of her face. "You have to trust me, Kate."

"I do, Alec. Really. And now that we've got that settled, I'd be forever grateful if you'd please just leave me alone to die in peace."

She might not be going to die, Alec thought as he walked to the shower hut. But she was damn well going to feel that way. He looked up at the sky, which was a benevolent blue this morning. But he knew all too well that this lush land was like a beautiful, fickle woman, full of lies and false promises. He should have been on the river two hours ago, but waking up in the hammock with his wife in his arms had felt too good, too right.

"It's only one day," he told himself as he soaped down, washing away the redolent scent of their love-making that still clung to his skin. "The gold has been under all that mud this long. It can stay buried a little while longer."

As he toweled off, Alec wondered if the concoction Rafael had first made for him after a night of pub-crawling back at Oxford had kicked in yet. If he was going to lose a day of treasure hunting, he might as well spend it in other pleasurable pursuits. And he knew just where to start.

# 15

K.J. WAS AMAZED and extremely relieved that the horrid concoction Alec had forced upon her had actually cleared her head and settled her stomach by the time he returned from the shower.

"Now I understand why the drug companies are searching for cures down here," she said after her own shower. "If that drink was any example of the potential, Rafael's tribe is going to end up very, very rich. Although," she added, "I do think they'll have to work a bit on taste and color."

"Good point," he agreed.

She was surprised when she felt no morning-after nervousness with Alec. In fact, as they shared a late breakfast of fruit, tortillas, delicious rich dark coffee and the ubiquitous manioc, K.J. felt almost as if they'd been beginning their day this way for the past year of their marriage. It seemed so comfortable. So right.

After breakfast, lying together in the hammock while the rain tapped a brisk staccato on the roof overhead, Alec told her all about the expedition, going into detail about the log, the old parchment map, the rumors of buried treasure that had circulated throughout this region for five centuries. K.J. could not have been more enthralled if he'd been reading to her from one of his novels.

"That's fascinating."

"It's pretty much the same thing I told you that night."

"Really?" She cuddled closer. He was wearing another of the soft, faded chambray shirts, but had left it open, allowing her to press a light kiss against his hard, dark chest. "I think, in the interest of full disclosure, it's time I admit that I didn't hear much of anything you said that night." Except that he'd wanted her. She'd certainly had no trouble hearing that!

Without the controlling factors of a hair dryer and stiff brush, her hair had dried into a riotous mass of curls. He tugged a long strand of silky red hair past her shoulders, then released it, watching as it sprung back into a loose spiral.

"I don't understand. You certainly seemed to be listening. In fact, I seem to remember thinking you were fixated on the story."

"Actually, I was fixated on making love with you."

His fingers, which had been playing in her hair, stilled momentarily. "Well, I suppose there could be worse reasons for you not catching the details." She could feel his deep, rumbling chuckle against the cheek that was resting on his bare chest. "So, now that you're all up-to-date on the particulars, do you have any suggestions on how to spend the rest of the day?"

Her scold tried to remind her that they really needed to work on the plans for their divorce. Not wanting to think of that right now, when she was right where she wanted to be, in Alec's arms, K.J. ruthlessly shut it off and refused to listen.

"I suppose I could come up with one or two." She smiled up at him as her hand inched down his torso. "Since it's raining too hard to risk going out on the river."

"And to think, before you arrived in Santa Clara, I

was beginning to hate this monsoon weather." He grinned down at her as he rolled over and pressed himself against her.

K.J. combed her fingers through his dark hair as she lifted her lips to his.

For a long blissful time, the only sound in the hut was the tap tap tap of the rain on the roof and the music of loving words and soft sighs.

Since they couldn't make love all of the time, in the afternoon Alec returned to his desk, where he began charting out the next day's search course while K.J. lost herself in Rafael's book again. She was nearly at the end when something struck her.

"Alec!"

"Mmm?" He didn't look up from his map.

"It says here that the old tribes once performed sacrifices to their ancient gods."

"Sure." He shrugged and calculated variables. "Some still do, which explains some of the fetishes you see tied to the stakes outside various huts."

"Sometimes the sacrifices were human."

"Again, that's not so surprising. Lots of ancient cultures had human sacrifice as part of their religious doctrine. Including the Celts," he said, reminding her of the violent history of their ancestors' native Scotland.

"There's a story in here about a multiple sacrifice. To appease a god referred to as the sleeping giant. Apparently, whenever he sensed that the people weren't being respectful enough, or feared him, he'd wake up. It says his temper was so horrible that when he roared the earth would shake and fire would fall from the sky."

"We're in the Ring of Fire here, Kate. I'd imagine

there are hundreds of myths dealing with volcanoes and earthquakes."

"I'd imagine so," she agreed. "But how many of those do you think have to do with the giant's revenge against murderous monsters created from silver and their treasure trove of stolen gold?"

She'd finally captured his full attention. Alec put down his pencil and came back over to the hammock. "Monsters created from silver?"

"That's what it says." She handed him the book and watched silently as he read the brief vengeance myth.

"The silver could be Spanish armor," he mused.

"That's exactly what I was thinking. And, of course, they would have murdered the Incas to have gotten the gold in the first place, which fits the description."

"And the mudslide could have come from a volcano's eruption. But you'd think the captain would have mentioned that little detail."

"He wasn't writing a novel, Alec. He was just putting the information, as he knew it, into his log. And I would imagine that he would have been in a bit of a hurry to get out of port if a volcano was erupting. Which would tend to make his journal entry a little sketchy."

Alec rubbed his jaw. "That's possible, I suppose. And it's also more than possible that this refers to our barge. But it's just another confirmation of the original story of the lost gold."

If K.J. had been surprised at how right it felt to be with Alec this way, she was amazed at the little thrill that skimmed through her when he referred to the missing treasure as "our barge." As if they'd become a team.

"It's more than just a confirmation." She was also

more than a little pleased that she might have uncovered an important clue.

"How's that?" She looked almost as pleased with herself as she looked after lovemaking, Alec thought. Her eyes were gleaming and bright scarlet flags of emotion waved high on her cheekbones.

"It's the giant. I saw him yesterday."

"Before or after you overindulged in that pupunha?"

She lifted her chin in that challenging way that made him want to kiss her. "Before. When we came out of that slot canyon into the marshy lake."

"So now we're talking about the monster from the black lagoon?"

"I wish you'd be serious," she huffed. "I'll also expect an apology after I've led you to your treasure."

Alec was about to tell her that he'd already found his treasure, that she meant more to him than a king's ransom of gold, when her words sunk in.

"You think you know where it is? After being here two days?"

"If you want to get technical, I've been here three days. And yes, I think I know. It's on the other side of that lake, Alec. Right below the mountain. The one that looks like a sleeping giant."

Alec stared at her for a long suspended time. Then cursed. Then reached down and pulled her up to him. "I love you, you gorgeous, sexy, intelligent woman!"

As he kissed her breathless, K.J. reminded herself that he was only using the *L* word in its general sense. He probably would have said the same thing to anyone who may have solved his puzzle for him. Rafael, perhaps. Or Raul, the boatman. Or even that toothless old woman who'd danced next to her for a time at the festival last night.

"You really think this is it?" she asked when they finally surfaced for air.

"I really think it is," he confirmed with that bold buccaneer's grin that could always send her heart tumbling. He shot a quick, impatient look up at the ceiling. "Too bad it's pouring."

"I suppose it would be too dangerous to go out on the river now."

"Dangerous, stupid and downright deadly," he agreed. "However, since the gold hasn't gone anywhere in five centuries, it'll still be there tomorrow. In the meantime—" he gathered her tighter as they both fell back down onto the hammock "—we might as well kill a little time while I give you a finder's reward."

"Again?" She arched her neck as his lips skimmed a path of electricity down her throat. "So soon?"

"Hey—" his fingers flicked open the buttons on the khaki-colored camp shirt she'd bought at Banana Republic "—we've got a lot of lost time to make up for."

Refusing to dwell on the past, and unwilling to contemplate a future without this man, K.J. laughed and surrendered to the moment. To her husband.

WANTING TO GET an early start in the morning, they woke at dawn. Not that they'd gotten all that much sleep. K.J. discovered Alec hadn't been kidding about making up for lost time. Not that she'd had any objection. On the contrary, she'd proven every bit as sexually hungry, which, as she stretched out the kinks from the rigorous exercise she wasn't accustomed to, still continued to surprise her.

She would have thought that once they'd made love—once they'd gotten all those months of dreaming and fantasizing out of their minds—the need would have lessened. But instead, it seemed that each time they made love only had K.J. wanting Alec even more.

She pondered over that all the way back up the river, through the slot canyon, and then finally across the lake to the base of the mountain. As she looked a long, long way up at it and imagined how it must have looked raining fire and ash and molten lava down on the invading conquistadores, K.J. could only hope that all Alec's guidebooks were right about the volcano now being dormant.

This time they hadn't come alone. Following in dug-out canoes outfitted with motors, identical to the one she'd taken to the village, were several men who had strong backs for digging through layers of mud, and an apparent unwavering loyalty to Alec. Which wasn't at all surprising, K.J. thought, watching how he treated them with the same respect he would an Oxford don.

They hadn't talked much during the trip; Alec had been occupied steering the boat and studying his maps and charts, while K.J. had busied herself taking more photographs. The scenery was as exotic and dazzling as her previous trip, but this time she took just as many shots of this man who'd complicated her life. The same man, her scold reminded her, that she'd promised to bring back to New York with her. As a bachelor.

Still uneasy about alligators, snakes and piranhas, K.J. was more than willing to wait on deck while Alec and the other men waded through the marshy water at the base of the sleeping giant. Several, Alec included, wielded metal detectors.

After a time, he stopped and compared the markings on the parchment to the modern maps, then looked up at the mountaintop again.

"Okay," he finally said. His voice was calm, but K.J., who'd come to know her husband a great deal better over the past few days, could hear the repressed excitement in it. "Let's try here."

She watched as one of the men set small charges designed to move the top layers of mud. Watched with her heart in her throat as the men brought out the metal detectors again. Then felt her own shoulders sag as they failed to turn up any sign of the barge. Or the gold.

Three more attempts in locations nearby also proved fruitless. K.J. followed Alec's glance up toward the sky, where the familiar anvil clouds had begun to gather.

"We've got time for one more shot," he decided. He waded about a hundred yards away, checked the readings on his hand-held G.P.S. and instructed the man to set the plastic charge.

There was a low rumble. Mud flew into the air, accompanied by the complaint of giant blue herons that, finally tiring of the humans, took wing. Once again the detectors came out. Once again K.J. heard the curses muttered in Spanish, Portuguese and Indian. But revealing that almost inhuman patience that made his lovemaking so remarkable, Alec seemed to be taking this failure in stride, as he had the others.

Just when she was about to accept that she hadn't really helped him after all, she saw every muscle in his body tense. He ran the metal detector back over the spot he'd just checked. Then again.

K.J.'s patience was not nearly as strong as his. "Did you find something?" she called out, leaning over the rail of the boat.

"Maybe." Mindless of the muck, he crouched down

and began digging with his bare hands. "But it could be just some fisherman's knife. Or a lost watch."

The other men, caught up in the air of suspense that suddenly hung over them even thicker than the building humidity, also began digging. On the boat, K.J. was holding her breath.

She felt a raindrop on her face. Then another. "No," she pleaded to whatever gods or fates controlled this strange, almost unearthly place. "Not yet. Please." As she felt more moisture on her face, K.J. scrubbed at it with her hands and realized that her tangled nerves were making her cry.

A shout in Spanish suddenly rung out over the distant rumble of thunder. Another. Then another. As K.J. watched in both disbelief and amazement, one of the men held up what appeared to be a mud-encrusted bowl. Another produced a coin. Then suddenly, everyone was shouting and laughing and waving booty in the air.

Putting aside any fears of unsavory wildlife lurking in the murky waters, K.J. leaped over the tarnished brass railing and ran toward Alec, her booted feet making sucking sounds as she forced them through the muck and mire.

She flung her arms around his neck, almost knocking him over. He lifted her up and they were kissing and laughing, and kissing some more as the rain mingled with the tears streaming down K.J.'s wet face. Tears no longer born of tension, but of joy.

K.J. would have given anything to stop time at that glorious moment. Unfortunately, she'd already discovered that the hands of time inexorably moved forward. A fact that was brought home when they all returned to the village and found Rafael waiting at the dock.

"Congratulations, Alec." He hugged his friend, seeming unconcerned that his white gauze shirt was now covered with red-brown mud. "The good news has preceded you. You actually have found the treasure."

"I have." Alec's answer was directed at Rafael, but his gaze was on Kate.

"Is it everything you hoped?"

"Better." His eyes met hers and held. "Infinitely better."

"Well, I'm pleased." Rafael's grin backed up that assertion. "And I have more good news."

"Oh?"

"I have been in contact with my friends in the government. For a small donation to the new judicial building, they're prepared to grant you a divorce tomorrow. If you still want one, that is."

"You'll have to ask Kate that question." Alec's deep voice was devoid of emotion, giving K.J. not a single clue as to how he felt.

Rafael turned toward her, his brown eyes solicitous. "Kate?"

Her mind was whirling, as it had been doing so much of the time since her arrival in this country. Part of her yearned to say no, that she'd changed her mind, that she wanted to spend the rest of her life with Alec. If only he'd say something!

"I suppose, despite today's excitement, not much has changed," she said flatly. Once again she waited for Alec to say something—anything. Once again he remained stubbornly silent. She met his enigmatic gray eyes, which had looked at her with such warmth and emotion, but were now giving absolutely nothing away. It was as if a steel curtain had come down between them. "Are you still willing to come to New York for the auction?"

"I said I would," he reminded her.

"Yes." She dragged a hand through her mud-encrusted hair. "And it is supposed to be a bachelor auction."

"Which I suppose makes a divorce a logistical necessity."

"Yes." Tears stung. She resolutely blinked them away. "Well, I think, now that we've gotten that settled, I'll go take a shower. I must be wearing about a century's worth of mud."

He didn't answer, only nodded. As she turned away, K.J. wondered if she'd imagined that dark shadow of disappointment she'd seen move across his eyes.

Although they didn't say another word about the divorce, that night their bodies were eloquent as they made love with silent desperation.

The following morning, as they flew out of the village on a small six-seater commuter plane, Alec turned toward her. "I didn't say anything last night, because quite honestly, I had other things on my mind. But I want you to know how much I appreciate your help in finding the gold."

K.J. shrugged. "I didn't do that much," she said flatly, fingering the necklace of polished native nuts Rafael had given her as a going-away present.

"Of course you did. You provided the key, Kate. Which is why I'm giving you half the profits after the government gets its split."

Her mind had been mired in the depressing thought of their upcoming divorce. Once again, he managed to surprise her. "That isn't necessary."

"Of course it is." He took hold of her hand and

laced their fingers together in a casual, easy gesture that belied the fact that they were on their way to the capital city to dissolve their marriage. "I was running out of time, Kate. I couldn't have done it without you."

"Well, I appreciate the gesture, even if it isn't necessary." Perhaps, she considered, added to her inheritance, along with the money she knew she'd make from the sale of her Amazonian photographs, her share of the Inca gold would allow her to turn in her resignation and work on her photography full time. "I realize that you haven't had any time to really examine the treasure. But do you have a ballpark figure—?"

"I'd say about a million."

"A million?" She stared up at him, convinced she must have heard wrong. "A million dollars?"

"That's a conservative estimate. My educated guess is that it'll go a lot higher. Pre-Columbian stuff, ugly as most of it is, is pretty popular. And the fact that so much of it is gold and silver makes it even more valuable."

"I can't believe it. Are you saying I could end up with several hundred thousand dollars?"

"No, I'm saying that your share will be at least a million dollars."

Her mind was reeling. Although she'd always prided herself on her imagination, there was no way K.J. could begin to comprehend being a millionaire.

"I'll be able to quit my job."

"Heck, if it goes as high as it could, you might be able to buy the company," he said with the first warm, Alec grin she'd witnessed since they'd arrived back in Santa Clara yesterday afternoon.

"I won't have to worry about getting a promotion."

"I wouldn't think so," he agreed.

Which meant, K.J. thought, that it wouldn't really matter if she didn't bring this Heart hero bachelor back to the auction. What could they do? Fire her after she'd already quit?

If it were only that easy. "I guess, since the money obviously changes things, I should let you off the hook. About the auction."

"I'll admit I'm not exactly looking forward to it. And I'd love an excuse to bail out on the entire scheme." His thumb was absently stroking the sensitive flesh of her palm, creating that all-too-familiar tingling sensation. "But I can't see your sense of honor allowing you to back down on a promise. Even one you didn't originally initiate."

"You know me that well." It was not a question, but a quietly stated admission. K.J. also was uncomfortable thinking that's exactly what she was doing by turning her back on her marriage vows.

"Not in the beginning. But we've gotten a lot closer these past few days, Kate. Close enough for me to get a handle on how your mind works."

She wondered what he'd say if she told him that her mind was working just fine, but her heart was desperately broken.

"So you're still willing to come back with me to New York?"

"Absolutely." He lifted their joined hands to his lips and kissed that tender skin his caress had stimulated. "I may be willing to go back to bachelor status for you, Kate. But I still haven't had my fill of you. Which means you're not going to get rid of me quite yet."

Although she could feel that traitorous sting of tears behind her eyes, Kate smiled at that, finding his sexy threat more thrilling than the remarkable idea that she was about to be a millionaire.

# 16

*New York City*

IT WAS A night designed for romance. The national flags flying in front of the famed Waldorf-Astoria revealed that the Sultan of Brunei, the Prince of Wales and the prime minister of Canada were currently guests of the luxurious hotel.

But on this special night, not one of the women gathered in the gilded ballroom was interested in politics or celebrities. Although all had their own personal reasons for attending the bachelor auction, the electric mood revealed that most had arrived determined to win—at least for one unforgettable date—a bachelor hunk. A true romance-novel hero, the embossed and gilt-edged invitations had promised.

"So, how are you doing?" Molly asked K.J. as they sat side by side at the damask-draped table the editorial staff had booked for the occasion. The first three bachelors had already been auctioned off, earning hefty contributions to the literacy charity.

"Fine." The way K.J. spoke through a tightly clenched jaw said otherwise.

"Any regrets?"

"No." At Molly's knowing look, she sighed and shook her head. "That's a lie. I have about a gazillion and one regrets." And that was just for starters. Yet the one thing she'd never repent was that glorious time she'd spent with Alec in the jungle.

She'd no sooner spoken than the emcee at the front of the room introduced "Heart Books's own Indiana Jones."

"Well, I can certainly understand the reason for a gazillion of those regrets," Molly murmured as Alec took center stage. "What I can't understand is why you let a hunk like that get away."

"That's easy to answer." Since she was already feeling intoxicated enough, K.J. ignored the wine the waiter had poured and took a long sip of ice water she hoped would calm her jangled nerves. It didn't. "Sometimes I can be really, really stupid."

"Well, there's always one solution. You can buy him back."

K.J.'s fingers tightened even more on her bag. The bag that held her royal blue CitiBank savings passbook. "That's exactly what I'm going to do."

She'd suspected the moment she walked into the cantina that she'd made a mistake in deciding to get a divorce. By the time they'd made love for the first time, she'd known that she didn't want to let Alec go. Unfortunately, her stiff Campbell pride hadn't allowed her to tell him how much she loved him. Also complicating the situation had been that sometimes irksome honor, drilled into her first by her father, then honed by her grandmother, that had required her to provide the hero she'd promised.

But last night, after they'd made love for the first time in her bed, K.J. had decided to do whatever it took—even grovel, if it came down to that—to convince Alec that they belonged together. And not just for a few hot, passionate nights, or even a shared treasure-seeking adventure. What she wanted, K.J. had realized, was a lifetime with this man. Wherever it took them.

K.J. managed, just barely, to restrain her irritation as the emcee went on and on, extolling Alec Mackenzie's many attributes—his fame, his fortune, his hard male body—the same way she might have introduced a Chippendale dancer.

When women at nearby tables began murmuring in feminine appreciation, it took a herculean effort for K.J. to tamp down her temper and resist leaping up and telling all those would-be bidders that this particular hero was already taken. Even the description of the date—that less-than-comfort-class expedition to Lapland—didn't seem to deter interest in the dashing treasure hunter.

Not that she could really blame them, she admitted reluctantly. He looked so good. So gorgeous. So damn self-confident. If she hadn't known how much he had dreaded this auction, K.J. would have almost believed he was enjoying himself when he flashed that wicked warrior's smile that had a roomful of women screaming like adolescent girls at a Hanson concert.

"We'll begin the bidding at one thousand dollars," the emcee announced.

That bid was instantly matched by a blonde seated in the front of the room.

"Fifteen hundred," a brunette called from the balcony.

"Two thousand," another blonde said before the brunette could even sit down.

K.J. was not surprised when the numbers steadily climbed. When a bidder paused at twenty thousand, she realized she was in danger of losing Alec. It was time to act.

She leaped to her feet, still clutching her bag. "Twenty thousand five hundred."

"Twenty thousand seven hundred and fifty." The determined brunette was wearing a spray-painted leopard print dress and enough makeup to stock Bloomingdale's entire cosmetic department.

"Twenty thousand eight hundred." K.J. countered.

"Twenty thousand nine hundred." Even from this distance, K.J. could see the flinty determination in the woman's kohl-lined eyes.

"Thirty thousand one hundred and forty two dollars." It was, less some change, the bottom line in her passbook.

"Thirty-five thousand," the other bidder said smugly, as if knowing she'd just outbid K.J. for the final time.

But K.J. had an ace in the hole. Actually, she thought, as she heard Molly's sympathetic murmur, a bargeful of aces. "One million thirty thousand one hundred and forty-two dollars." The entire audience gasped in unison. "And thirty-eight cents," K.J. added.

Unsurprisingly, there was nothing the brash brunette could say to that. K.J. tried not to gloat as she watched the woman sit back down.

"You realize," Molly said, "that you've just given away every cent you have."

"Ah, but I've definitely gotten more than my money's worth. And besides, I'm going to have a filthy rich husband."

Not that the money mattered. All that mattered was that they were going to be together. As they were meant to be.

As she made her way through the tables, toward the front of the room, toward Alec, K.J. felt as if she were looking through the lens of a camera. As her loving gaze focused on Alec, everything and everyone else in the room faded away, like wisps of morning fog.

And wonderfully, he was looking at her exactly the same way.

"Absolutely crazy," he murmured as she climbed the stairs to the stage.

"About you," she answered.

Just like that first night, in another banquet hall, they could have been the only two people in the room. They only had eyes for each other.

"Your scold's probably screaming bloody murder."

"I wouldn't know. I sent her away. For good."

"Clever lady." His warm gaze skimmed appreciatively over her. "I like that dress."

"Thank you." She smiled and, mindless of their rapt audience, twirled like a little girl showing off a new party dress. The red silk swirled around her thighs. "A man once bought it for me."

He lifted a dark brow. "A lover?"

She nodded. "But not just any lover." Her smile shone in her eyes. "A magnificent lover."

With that, he gathered her into his arms and kissed her. A long kiss brimming over with love and passion and promise. The kind of kiss designed to make every female in the room sigh with envy. Not that Alec or K.J. were paying any attention.

"We never had a honeymoon," he said when the glorious kiss finally came to an end.

"We'll have one in Lapland."

He grinned at this proof that she'd reclaimed her legacy. "I think we can do better than that. How about something more conventional? Like Tahiti. We can make love, stroll along beaches as white as snow make love, swim naked in tropical lagoons, make love, feed each other passion fruit...."

"To keep our strength up for making love," she guessed.

He plucked the ivory comb from her hair and watched it tumble over her bare shoulders in a fiery waterfall. "Absolutely. Lord, you are an intelligent woman, Mrs. Mackenzie."

"Speaking of that, to have a true honeymoon, we'll have to get remarried."

"That won't be necessary." He tugged on the end of a bright curl.

K.J. slapped his hand away. "I'm not settling for just sex, Alec, as terrific as it is." She put her hands on her hips and thrust her chin up at him. "I want it all."

Feeling remarkably carefree, considering they continued to be the center of attention, he laughed and gathered her back into his arms.

"Getting remarried isn't necessary because we never got divorced in the first place."

"But what about that nice little old man in the capital?" He'd been sitting at a small wooden table in the main square of the city, his notary seal at the ready. "We both signed the paper. And he stamped it...." Realization slowly dawned. "He was a fake, wasn't he?"

"It's a Catholic country, Kate. They don't have divorce."

"You lied. That entire trip to the capital was just a sneaky scheme cooked up by you and Rafael to keep me from getting my divorce!"

"True. And I'll admit that I felt a bit guilty about that. But I was desperate. And there was no way in hell I was going to let the woman I loved—the only woman I'll ever love—get away again."

"You love me?" She'd known that, of course. It was just nice hearing the words for the very first time.

"Absolutely." He kissed her lightly. Sweetly. "Positively." His lips punctuated his claim. "Forever and ever." He dipped into his pocket and took out a black velvet box.

"Oh, Alec, I love you, too," she breathed as he slipped the woven gold band back onto her finger where it belonged. Where it had always belonged. "Absolutely. Positively. Forever and ever." They could have been exchanging their marriage vows all over again.

"Amen," he said with a huge sigh of relief and pleasure. As he had that first night, and again at the festival, he lifted her into his arms and carried her off the stage. Still lost in one another, neither paid any attention to the thunderous applause.

A thought suddenly occurred to K.J. "Since you're still not a bachelor, it's certainly a good thing I bought you."

"I wasn't that worried. Since your friend had a back-up bundle of bucks in her purse."

"You gave Molly money to bid on you?"

"Only if you ran out of dough. Then she was going to hand me over to you."

"Well, you certainly seemed to have thought of everything."

"I'm yours, Kate. And I was willing to do whatever it took to keep it that way."

Since it was what she wanted, K.J. magnanimously decided to forgive them all—Alec, Rafael and Molly—for their various deceptions.

"Will we be going to Lapland after our honeymoon?" she asked.

Alec looked down at her, his expression as serious

as she'd ever seen it. "Only if you want to. Because I've recently discovered, albeit a little late, that the only treasure I really want—or need—is you."

"That's so sweet." She lifted a hand to his dark, rugged cheek. "And, of course, I want to go find your Viking ship with you, Alec." Her smile faded to a slight frown. "Although I suspect it'll be freezing in Lapland, which means we'll probably have to wear clothes."

"Don't count on it, Mrs. Mackenzie, since I intend to get you naked as often as possible. We'll just have to keep each other warm."

And as their lips met and clung in a kiss sweeter than any they'd shared before, K.J. had not a single doubt that was one vow neither she nor Alec would have any trouble keeping.

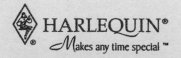

If you enjoyed what you just read,
then we've got an offer you can't resist!

# Take 2 bestselling love stories FREE!

# Plus get a FREE surprise gift!

---

**Clip this page and mail it to Harlequin Reader Service®**

| **IN U.S.A.** | **IN CANADA** |
|---|---|
| 3010 Walden Ave. | P.O. Box 609 |
| P.O. Box 1867 | Fort Erie, Ontario |
| Buffalo, N.Y. 14240-1867 | L2A 5X3 |

**YES!** Please send me 2 free Harlequin Temptation® novels and my free surprise gift. Then send me 4 brand-new novels every month, which I will receive months before they're available in stores. In the U.S.A., bill me at the bargain price of $3.12 plus 25¢ delivery per book and applicable sales tax, if any*. In Canada, bill me at the bargain price of $3.57 plus 25¢ delivery per book and applicable taxes**. That's the complete price and a savings of over 10% off the cover prices—what a great deal! I understand that accepting the 2 free books and gift places me under no obligation ever to buy any books. I can always return a shipment and cancel at any time. Even if I never buy another book from Harlequin, the 2 free books and gift are mine to keep forever. So why not take us up on our invitation. You'll be glad you did!

142 HEN CNEV
342 HEN CNEW

---

Name _____ (PLEASE PRINT)

---

Address _____ Apt.# _____

---

City _____ State/Prov. _____ Zip/Postal Code _____

\* Terms and prices subject to change without notice. Sales tax applicable in N.Y.
\*\* Canadian residents will be charged applicable provincial taxes and GST.
All orders subject to approval. Offer limited to one per household.
® are registered trademarks of Harlequin Enterprises Limited.

TEMP99                                    ©1998 Harlequin Enterprises Limited

# Tough, rugged and irresistible...

### THE
# AUSTRALIANS

Stories of romance Australian-style, guaranteed to
fulfill that sense of adventure!

## This March 1999 look for
# *Boots in the Bedroom!*
## by **Alison Kelly**

Parish Dunford lived in his cowboy boots—no one was going
to change his independent, masculine ways. Gina, Parish's
newest employee, had no intention of trying to do so—she pre-
ferred a soft bed to a sleeping bag on the prairie. Yet somehow she couldn't stop thinking of how those boots would look
in her bedroom—with Parish still in them....

*The Wonder from Down Under: where spirited women win
the hearts of Australia's most independent men!*

Available March 1999
at your favorite retail outlet.

# HARLEQUIN®
*Makes any time special* ™

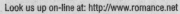

# COMING NEXT MONTH

**#721 SINGLE, SEXY…AND SOLD! Vicki Lewis Thompson**
**Bachelor Auction**

When firefighter Jonah Hayes rescued a puppy, he had no idea
he'd become a hero. Or that he'd end up on the auction block.
But when Natalie LeBlanc, the puppy's sexy owner, bid $33,000
for him, Jonah's desire to test the chemistry between them
went up in smoke. Not only was Natalie out of his league…
she was out of her mind!

**#722 UNLIKELY HERO Sandy Steen**

Loner Logan Walker wasn't the type to rescue damsels in
distress. But even *he* couldn't leave gorgeous Paige Davenport
stranded by the side of the road. He told himself it was only
for a short time—but Paige managed to worm her way into his
life…and his heart. Little did he know that Paige had already
left one groom at the altar.…

**#723 IN THE DARK Pamela Burford**
**The Wrong Bed**

Cat Seabright was expecting a friend who'd agreed to a "baby-
making date." All Brody Mikhailov expected was a warm bed
in New York City. And though a blackout threw everything
into confusion, both of them got what they were looking
for…in the dark.

**#724 PRIVATE LESSONS Julie Elizabeth Leto**
**Blaze**

Banker Grant Riordan was a bit of a stuffed shirt—until
"Harley" showed up and sent him reeling. The woman dressed
like an exotic dancer, had the eyes of an innocent…and didn't
know who she was! Grant considered her his every fantasy…
in the flesh. And while Harley searched for answers, Grant
learned some very *memorable* lessons.…